The Chocolate Box Holiday

Daphne Neville

ISBN: 978-0-244-91997-9

PublishNation, London
www.publishnation.co.uk

Other Titles by This Author

TRENGILLION CORNISH MYSTERY SERIES
The Ringing Bells Inn
Polquillick
Sea, Sun, Cads and Scallywags
Grave Allegations
The Old Vicarage
A Celestial Affair
Trengillion's Jubilee Jamboree

The Old Tile House

Chapter One

Late May 2016

In the back garden of her home near to the church in a quiet Northamptonshire village, Sandra Burton watered lobelia and fuchsias trailing from hanging baskets on either side of the kitchen window. She sang heartily as water dripped through the sphagnum moss and splashed onto the toes of her well-worn slippers. Life had never felt so good.

When the watering can was empty she put it back beneath the outside tap and with a spring in her step picked a sprig of parsley from the herb garden. As she approached the house, she heard the distinct thud of the fridge door slam shut followed by the rattling of glasses on the pantry shelf.

Inside the kitchen, Sandra found sixteen year old Zac biting into a large slice of cold pizza as he poured blackcurrant squash into a glass.

Her face broke into an exaggerated smile. "Hi, love, I didn't hear the bus. Where are the girls?"

"Dawdling as usual. Why?"

"Because I've something really exciting to tell you all."

Zac yawned. "Oh, I'm starving. What's for tea?"

"Fish."

"With chips?" Zac was hopeful.

"No, mashed potatoes and peas."

The front door opened and Zac's younger twin sisters walked into the hallway each dropping their school bags onto the floor. Both half-heartedly greeted their mother as they made for the kitchen cupboard containing chocolate bars and crisps.

Sandra reinstated her exaggerated smile. "Hi girls, I've some really exciting news for you all."

Both girls frowned.

"Oh," said Vicky, with little interest.

Kate, however, was curious. "So what is it, Mum?"

"I've won a prize in a competition."

Vicky groaned. "Not another toaster."

Sandra shook her head. "No, it's something much, much more exciting."

In anticipation the three children stood with their heads tilted to one side.

"Which is?" asked Zac, prompting his mother to speak.

Sandra took in a deep breath. "It's a holiday," she said, "a lovely holiday in Cornwall."

Kate's face lit up. "What! But that's brilliant, Mum. Please say it's Newquay and then Vicky and me can go surfing. One of the boys at school said there's a really good beach there with lots of sand and huge waves. Apparently it's really, really popular and they have a music and surfing festival there every summer."

Sandra shook her head. "Sorry, Kate, but no it's not. It's a place I've never heard of before on the south coast called Pentrillick. But don't worry, Cornwall's not that big so we'll still be able to go to Newquay from there."

Kate nodded to acknowledge her approval. "Sounds good. Well done, Mum, that's the best prize you've ever won." She poured herself a glass of blackcurrant squash. "So what does the holiday consist of? You know, is it a caravan, a hotel or what?"

"It's a cottage," said Sandra, pulling details of the competition prize from an envelope and passing it to the children. "See, a lovely chocolate box cottage. It's called Sea View."

"Wow! How many bedrooms does it have?" asked Vicky, eying a picture of the white-washed building.

"Four. One double which is en suite, two twin and one single."

Vicky rubbed her hands together. "Brilliant, that means you and Dad get the double and we'll all be able to have one each."

Sandra bit her bottom lip and slowly shook her head. "Well, actually, I'm afraid not. You girls will have to share, you see, because I've invited Great Auntie Hetty to join us and …"

2

"…and she's accepted?" Vicky groaned.

Sandra attempted to smother a smile. "Actually, you interrupted me before I'd finished. What I was trying to say was that Great Auntie Hetty will join us *and* Grandma too."

Sandra waited for a rebellious response but all three teenagers were rendered speechless. "But they won't be driving down the same day as us," she continued, "because Great Auntie Hetty's best friend's daughter is getting married on the day we go and so she'll drive down with Grandma on either the Sunday or the Monday."

"So…umm… when do we go?" asked Kate, feeling someone ought to say something positive as she reached for the biscuit tin.

"Saturday, August the sixth until the twenty seventh."

Zac gulped. "That means we'll be there for three weeks. Does Dad know yet?"

Sandra nodded. "Of course, I rang him as soon as I got the letter and I must say he's delighted. It was his idea to invite Great Auntie Hetty and Grandma."

Vicky groaned. "I might have known."

"I think you're being a little unfair, Vicky. Both Great Auntie Hetty and Grandma can be very good company and Grandma has been very low lately. She took losing Granddad very badly, poor soul."

"Yes, but they're just so straight-laced," said Vicky, breaking open a bag of salt and vinegar crisps, "especially Grandma. She believes children should be seen and not heard. Which is silly and shouldn't apply to us because we're teenagers now."

Sandra threw back her head and laughed. "Straight-laced! May I remind you that your grandmother and great aunt were teenagers back in the Swinging Sixties? I've seen pictures of them all made up and wearing mini skirts and a couple of lovely looking girls they were too."

Vicky dunked a crisp into her glass of squash. "Humph! But the Swinging Sixties were forever ago, Mum. Blimey, you weren't even born then."

Bill Burton finished his shift at the supermarket where he worked and crossed the car park to his faithful old Volvo Estate. Happily he whistled and merrily he took a hop, a skip and a jump, for not since he was a boy waking up on a Christmas morning had he felt so ecstatic, so jubilant. The reason being, the phone call from Sandra, his wife. Her news had set his mouth into a grin that he was unable to wipe from his clean-shaven face.

Because money was a little tight the family had not pre-booked a summer holiday but had instead planned to hire a tent and go camping wherever the weather looked the most promising when the time was right. But now that wouldn't be necessary for due to his wife's dedication and addiction to entering competitions they had something much, much better to look forward to. Three whole weeks in Cornwall. Bill started the Volvo's engine, switched on the car radio and heartily sang at the top of his voice, all the way home.

During the following weeks the family read as much as they were able on the Internet about Pentrillick and even borrowed books about Cornwall from the library. Bill looked forward to walking the cliff paths, doing a spot of sea fishing and enjoying a pint in the local pub. Sandra was keen to visit some of the locations where the BBC's television series *Poldark* had been filmed. She also planned to do a spot of sun bathing and looked forward to the prospect of eating out. The girls were really excited about surfing and swimming hence their parents were thrilled to discover that both wet suits and surf boards could be hired from Newquay which negated the expense of kitting the girls out. Zac wasn't sure what he wanted from the holiday. He wasn't one for sun bathing, he didn't much care for swimming and certainly not surfing, nor was he attracted to the notion of fishing, and he didn't think there would be many opportunities to chat up girls with Great Auntie Hetty and Grandma in tow. He did, however, like to draw and so made a mental note to make sure he packed a sketch pad or two and a selection of pencils.

Two weeks before the family were due to leave for their holiday, the children broke up from school. The weather during the last few days of term was glorious with temperatures well over thirty degrees Centigrade but sadly it did not last. Heavy thunderstorms brought the mini-heatwave to an abrupt end and the summer vacation began on a more moderate footing with temperatures hovering around average for the time of year.

On Saturday evening, Sandra switched on the television to watch the early evening news and on seeing the headlines, she tutted. "Goodness me. Look at this, Bill. What a nightmare."

Bill, half way through writing an email, unwillingly looked up from his laptop and Zac likewise glanced up from his mobile phone. The girls were upstairs in their bedroom.

Bill frowned. "Dear, dear, thank goodness we're not stuck in that lot," he said, observing aerial footage of stationary vehicles and their frustrated passengers queueing for miles in order to reach Dover and ferries to transport them over the Channel to France.

"Poor, poor souls," said Sandra, genuinely sympathetic, "it must be misery for families with young children. What a horrible way to start a holiday."

"I don't even want to think about it," said Bill, as his eyes wandered back to his laptop, "Thank goodness we're staying in this country."

Everyone lost interest in the News when it moved on to the subject of a possible ban for Russian athletes at the Rio Olympic Games but their interest was instantly regained when they heard mention of the name Pentrillick.

Sandra quickly grabbed the remote control and turned up the volume as all eyes focused on the television screen. Someone had been murdered in the village and the body had been discovered by Rosie Rutherford, a local artist, who apparently lived next door to the deceased.

No-one in the family spoke as the news sank in and Sandra turned the volume back down. From the girls' bedroom directly overhead, the sound of music echoed through the house and the remainder of the television News fell on deaf ears.

Zac spoke first. His face was white. "Does that mean there is a murderer on the loose at the place where we're going for our holiday?"

"Hmm, er…yes," said Sandra, "it looks very much as though that is the case."

Zac clearly felt uneasy. "But will it be safe?"

"Don't worry, son," said Bill, in a matter-of-fact manner, "I expect it'll turn out to be a domestic, these things usually are and I daresay the murderer will be under lock and key long before we set foot in Cornwall."

"But we go in two weeks," persisted Zac. "In fact two weeks today."

"And that's more than long enough for the police to have caught the killer. Isn't that so, Mother?"

Sandra frowned. It was obvious her husband was trying not to alarm their son. "I suppose so," she said. But her voice lacked conviction and she clearly shared Zac's apprehension.

Over the following two weeks, the family heard no more news regarding the murder in Pentrillick and so hoped, as Bill had suggested, a satisfactory arrest had been made. To build up the excitement, they made lists of things they needed to take with them. Sandra had her hair cut and restyled and they all went shopping and bought new clothing with the money they had saved up for the hiring of camping equipment and to pay campsite fees should they have gone on the camping holiday as originally planned.

Zac was also treated to a new quality sketch pad and the girls asked for a DVD entitled *Surfing for Beginners*. They considered buying sun cream but after watching the grey clouds rolling overhead decided instead to buy it in Cornwall, should it be needed. After all in Britain, summer could not always be relied upon to live up to its name.

On Friday morning, the day before they were due to leave, Sandra was delighted to watch the forecast and see that the weather looked settled for at least the first few days of their holiday.

On the washing line in the back garden she hung out a few last minute garments which blew nicely in the light south easterly breeze. With the back door and windows wide open to let in the welcome sunshine, she and the children then gathered together everything they needed to take with them and stood it all in the hallway ready to pack into the car when Bill arrived home from work.

In the evening the family sat in the living room together and watched the television, although no-one was really interested in anything they saw as they were too excited about the holiday.

At half past ten, the twins went to bed. Sandra and Bill followed soon after. Zac also went to his room but not with any intention of sleeping for he was determined to watch the opening ceremony of the Rio Olympic Games on the television set in his room. But gradually he snuggled down lower and lower beneath the bedclothes and long before Team GB walked into the arena, he was fast asleep.

Chapter Two

Very early on the morning of Saturday August the sixth, the Burton family left their Northamptonshire home for the drive to Cornwall. The sun was shining and the family were in very high spirits, even Vicky whose turn it was to sit in the middle of the back seat for the first part of the journey.

Because they were making good time, and she was aware that the cottage would not be available for their occupation until four o'clock, Sandra suggested they drove into Exeter when they came off the M5 to have some lunch and to stretch their legs.

Amongst the shops they found a small café in a backstreet where the prices seemed reasonable and so they went inside and seated themselves around an oblong table in a corner.

As the children looked at the menu, Sandra observed a painting hanging on the wall behind Bill. It was a rugged beach scene and in the bottom corner, two little penguins sat on a rock each wearing brightly coloured waistcoats. A small plaque on the frame informed her it was the work of Rosie Rutherford.

"Why do I know that name?" Sandra asked, waving her finger at the painting.

Bill turned to look up at it. "Hmm, I don't know but I must admit the name does sound familiar."

Zac gave the painting a cursory glance. "She's the artist who found the dead body of her neighbour in Pentrillick."

Sandra shuddered. "Oh dear, of course it is, silly me. I do hope they've found out who murdered that poor lady."

"I expect they have," said Bill, in a level-headed manner, "because we've heard no more about it, have we?"

"I think it's all very exciting," said Vicky, as she passed the menu to her mother, "going somewhere where there's been a murder, I mean."

Sandra took the menu and placed it on the table so that Bill might see it also. "That's because you're so young, Vicky. When you're older you'll see things differently. I can assure there is absolutely nothing exciting about death and especially murder."

"I must admit I rather like her style," said Bill, pointing at the painting and eager to change the subject. "I wouldn't mind having something like that above our fireplace."

Sandra nodded. "Yes, I agree and I suppose we might be able to see some of her work while we're in Cornwall but I should imagine it'll be way out of our price range."

Just after five o'clock, the family Volvo turned left off the A394 and into a country lane which ran downhill. Vicky excitedly waved her arm as they passed a farm and turned a sharp corner. "I just got a glimpse of the sea," she squeaked, "Really, I did and I've gone all goosepimply."

"Well, we must be nearly there," said Bill, taking his foot off the accelerator as they neared a tractor slowing down to turn into a field. "The signpost back on the main road said two miles."

Pentrillick was a large village, its main street ran parallel with the coast but from the road much of the sea was hidden behind cottages and houses which lined the narrow winding street.

Driving slowly through, they passed an antique shop, a hairdressers, and a large white building standing back from the road with a name-board saying Pentrillick Hotel. As they neared a church on the right-hand-side, Sandra waved her hands. "Slow right down, Bill. We must be nearly there because according to the brochure the cottage is almost opposite the church."

"There it is," shouted Vicky. "I recognise it from the picture."

The white-washed cottage stood well back from the road on a bend and opposite a sheltered bus stop. Bill drove into a parking space which ran alongside the front garden where pink roses grew over a metal arch framing the white front door. The children, eager to explore, jumped out before he had even turned off the ignition.

As per the accommodation instructions, the family followed a path around the side of the house and onto a patio which led into the back garden where a mass of summer flowering perennials and annuals took away Sandra's breath. Hollyhocks, lupins, roses,

9

dahlias, alstroemeria and sweet williams, all grew closely together in beds around a lush green lawn, and beyond the garden, the sea sparkled for miles until it blended into the distant horizon.

From beneath a tub of golden marigolds, Sandra pulled out a bunch of keys and unlocked the door of a sunny conservatory which led into one of the two reception rooms. Across the hallway was a dining room and next to it, the kitchen. Upstairs, two of the four bedrooms faced the sea and the other two were on the roadside next to the bathroom.

While Bill and Zac fetched luggage and provisions from the car, the girls ran from room to room squealing their approval. From the landing window they could see the colourful flower beds and the lawn, beyond which was a paved area bordered by a wrought iron fence and a gate which opened out onto a steep path which led to the beach below.

In a cupboard beneath the stairs, the twins found shelves neatly stacked with board games and colourful buckets, spades and a beach ball.

"Cluedo," laughed Vicky, "Haven't played that for years."

"And Scrabble," said Sandra looking over the shoulders of her daughters, "excellent, that will give us something to do if the weather is miserable."

"And Monopoly too," said Kate, "Dad likes to play that because he always wins."

"And I we must build sandcastles," said Vicky, picking up the buckets, "just like we did when we were little."

When it seemed that everything was out of the car, Bill went back out to make sure that nothing had been left behind before he locked it. He then crossed the road and looked in both directions to weigh up the location. To the left of Sea View Cottage lay a row of six terraced houses. They had no front gardens and their front doorsteps were on the edge of the narrow pavement. To the right of the cottage stood two semi-detached bungalows, both painted brilliant white and dazzling in the bright sun. Next to the bungalows was a chapel which on looking closer Bill realised was no longer used for religious purposes but was a community centre.

Further down the road he could see a post office and a fish and chip shop. He knew that somewhere in the village there was also a pub called the Crown and Anchor but as it was not visible and they had not passed it when driving into village, he assumed that it was further down the road and around the bend.

In the evening, as the family sat watching the Rio Olympic Games on television, all feeling sleepy after their journey and a walk along the beach, there was a knock on the front door. Sandra answered. On the doorstep stood a middle-aged lady holding a huge bunch of flowers.

"Hi, Mrs Burton?"

"Yes."

"Lovely to meet you. My name is Rosie and I'm calling on behalf of Lance Tait, the owner of this cottage. He asked me to bring you these flowers as a welcoming gift and to make sure that everything is satisfactory."

"Oh, that's very kind of you, Rosie," said Sandra, taking the flowers, "they're beautiful and everything is fine. In fact we're absolutely delighted with the cottage and its gorgeous location." She took a step backwards. "Would you like to come in?"

"No, no, I can't stop. I'm on my way to the pub to meet friends for dinner. Anyway, I hope you enjoy your stay. The weather is looking quite promising this week unlike the beginning of last week; Monday and Tuesday were ghastly, very wet and miserable." She pulled out a business card from her pocket. "If there are any problems please call me on this number and I'll get things sorted." She turned to leave. "Goodbye."

"Oh, yes, thank you, goodbye, err, Rosie."

As Sandra closed the door and walked back into the sitting room, she glanced at the card and the penny suddenly dropped. She gasped, slapped her forehead and tutted. "Oh, my goodness. It just didn't click with me who that was."

"So who was it?" Bill asked.

Sandra dropped the card onto a coffee table. "It was Rosie Rutherford the artist."

Vicky gasped. "You mean the very woman who found the dead body?"

Sandra nodded. "Yes, it must have been her."

"Cool," giggled Vicky.

"What did she look like?" Kate asked.

"Hmm, middle aged, attractive, well dressed, nice hair style. I'm not very good at describing people," Sandra admitted.

"No problem," said Bill, reaching for Sandra's laptop. "I'll Google her then we'll all be able to recognise her if we see her when out and about."

Sandra went into the kitchen where she found a large vase on the window sill and into it she carefully arranged the flowers. She then carried them back into the sitting room and placed them on the sideboard.

"Here's Rosie," said Bill, turning round the laptop for all to see. "I must admit, she's rather striking, and with auburn hair it shouldn't be difficult to pick her out in a crowd."

Chapter Three

Henrietta Tonkins, known to everyone as Hetty, stepped from the taxi as it pulled up in front of the two bed-roomed bungalow in Kettering, Northamptonshire in which she had lived for the past thirty years. Tired but happy, she tossed onto the kitchen table the hat she'd worn all day long at the wedding and kicked off her high-heeled shoes. After making a mug of tea she sat down on her leather settee, its seat warmed by the evening sun streaming in through the sitting room window. Thoughtfully she sipped her tea and pondered over the day's events. How beautiful the daughter of her best friend had looked in her wedding gown and how wonderful it was that she had finally married her childhood sweetheart.

Hetty put down her mug and looked through the pictures she had taken on her mobile phone. Everyone, young and old, looked so blissfully happy. With a wistful sigh she glanced at the ringless finger on her left hand and for a brief moment imagined herself as a young bride. For Hetty had never married; partly because no-one had ever swept her off her feet but mainly because no-one had ever asked her. There had been a few men in her life and of three she had been very fond, but none of the relationships had ever developed into anything serious. And so the years had passed and by the time she'd reached forty Hetty accepted the probability that she would always live alone. But she hadn't really minded, especially during the years when she had worked, in fact she had rather liked being footloose and fancy free and able to come and go as she pleased.

At the age of sixty two she retired from her lifelong occupation as a midwife; a job she had done for forty one years, and now two years on she confessed that time did sometimes drag. However, she managed to fill her days by reading novels on her Kindle, playing the piano and tending her modest garden. Through Facebook, she kept in touch with old work colleagues and some of the women whose babies she had delivered, and gradually her life had settled into a new but humdrum routine.

When her mug was empty Hetty picked up the house phone and rang her twin sister, Lottie, to relay last minute details of their trip to Cornwall the following day.

Charlotte Burton, known to everyone as Lottie, put down the phone after the call from her twin sister, glad that the final arrangements were made for their holiday in Cornwall. For Lottie, the younger of the twins by ten minutes, wasn't one to make spur of the moment decisions; she liked everything to be planned well in advance right down to the smallest of details. Hugh, her late husband, had been the same. He used to leave the house for work at the same time each morning, and they ate their dinner at the same time every evening. Television programmes were planned in advance and their children, Bill and Barbara, were brought up to know the importance of punctuality.

Lottie picked up the picture of her late husband, Hugh, taken on the day that he had retired. Tears filled her eyes. Poor Hugh, he'd hardly had a chance to enjoy his retirement before he was struck down with a massive stroke. Sadly, he was out alone when he'd collapsed in a nearby field where he had been picking mushrooms. By the time he was found, the damage had been done and he never regained consciousness.

Lottie put down the picture and thought about the trip to Cornwall. She had not been on a family holiday for twenty years or more. For soon after their son Bill had left home and married Sandra, their daughter Barbara who worked in advertising, was offered the chance of a job in America with the firm for whom she worked and she had seized it with enthusiasm. After that there had been just the two of them and their modest holidays were usually spent in Scotland or Wales.

At half past seven on Sunday morning, a taxi booked by Hetty, pulled up outside Lottie's semi-detached house in Barton Seagrave: its destination Kettering Railway Station. En route, it stopped to pick up Hetty from her bungalow.

The sun was already shining as the sisters waited on the station platform for the eight twenty train to London, St Pancras. It arrived on time and the sisters found their reserved seats and sat down opposite each other around a table.

When Hetty had first heard of the holiday, she said that she would drive to Cornwall but after some thought she decided it would be more enjoyable to go by train, especially if the sisters each purchased a senior citizens railcard which would enable them to get a substantial discount off the ticket price. Lottie, however, was a little unsure. She'd not travelled by train for many years and the prospect of crossing London alarmed her, but Hetty assured her the journey would be a piece of cake and there was no need for concern.

"You no doubt heard about the murder in the village we're going to stay at didn't you, Het?" said Lottie, as the train gathered speed.

Hetty nodded. "Hmm, I did and I've heard no more about it either. Have you?"

Lottie shook her head. "No, but I mentioned it to Bill when he phoned the other night because I was feeling a bit apprehensive. He said not to worry, but I do worry, I suppose it's being on my own now. I'm not used to the quiet, you see, especially in the middle of the night. I miss hearing Hugh breathing." She half-smiled. "I even miss his snoring. Not that he did that very often. It was only when he'd been to the pub and had a pint or two."

Hetty reached across the table and stroked her sister's hand. "It must be hard for you. Living alone after all these years, I mean. I'm used to it, of course and you never miss what you've never had. Do you see much of Bill and Sandra?"

Lottie nodded her head. "Not a lot but enough as I'm fully aware that Bill has his own family and his own life to lead. A job to keep down too. He pops in twice a week after work and Sandra calls in once a week and takes me shopping. I haven't seen the grandchildren for a while though, but then it's quite common for grandmothers to lose their appeal once youngsters reach their teens."

Hetty smiled. "Yes, I suppose so. Do Vicky and Kate still look identical?"

Lottie laughed. "Sadly yes. I always feel such a fool when I get them muddled up. Mum and Dad don't know how lucky they were having us look so different."

Hetty chuckled. "Hmm, but think of the tricks we could have played had we also been identical too."

"Yes, and I think that is a bit of a problem for Kate and Vicky's teachers, especially with the girls being dressed alike in school uniform."

Hetty and Lottie were chalk and cheese. Both were the same height, five feet and seven inches, but there the likeness ended. Hetty had brown eyes, Lottie's were green. Hetty was generously proportioned but not plump and Lottie was lean. In their younger days Lottie had light brown hair, it was now snow white, and Hetty had dark brown hair and with the help of hair dye it still was. Because she had worked with young people, Hetty liked to keep up with fashion, but Lottie gave up when her children were small. Hetty would never go out without make-up. Lottie only wore it on special occasions. Hetty played the piano but Lottie was musically tone deaf. Lottie liked knitting and sewing, but Hetty would struggle to stitch on a button. And over the years they had grown apart and their characters had gone in different directions too. In fact it was hard to believe they were even sisters let alone twins.

"How's Barbara?" Hetty asked, noticing a stray blob of nail varnish on the side of her thumb. "It's a shame she's so far away, it would be nice if you could see her more often."

"Ah, but she's happy living in America," said Lottie, "and if she's happy then I'm happy too. Besides, when she does come over for a visit it's always for a week or more, so I do still see quite a bit of her. And she phones me as regular as clockwork every Sunday."

"You really need to get on-line, Lottie. It would open up a whole new world for you and it'd be so much easier to keep in touch."

"Yes, well, one day maybe, but not just yet. I'm still struggling to come to terms with household things like insurance and suchlike. Hugh always took care of things like that, you see, but at least I have Bill to give a helping hand. Sandra too, she's on the ball with most things to do with running a home."

After arriving at St. Pancras Station the sisters took the tube to Paddington Station where they caught the ten fifty-seven train for Penzance which pulled into the West Country station at a quarter past four. Bill and Zac were waiting to greet the ladies as they stepped from the train.

"How lovely to have a railway station right beside the sea and at the end of the line as well," gushed Hetty, her hair ruffled and her cheeks glowing. "Lottie and I felt we were young again and we couldn't resist the temptation to hang our heads from the train windows to take in the gorgeous sea air."

Bill tutted. "Humph, that accounts for the wind swept hair then, and surely leaning from a train window is a very dangerous thing to do. If I remember correctly there are warning signs above the doors asking passengers to refrain from leaning out."

Hetty laughed awkwardly. "Well, when I say we hung our heads from the window I only mean a teeny-weeny little bit…not right out, so to speak."

Zac chuckled, amused to see that no-one was too old for a ticking-off from Dad.

"Okay," said Bill kissing his mother's cheek and hugging his Auntie Hetty. "Anyway, I'm glad you've both arrived safe and sound. And if you like it here then you'll love the cottage too. It's also right by the sea and at the bottom of the garden is a gate which opens onto the coastal path with steps leading down to the beach. We've only been here twenty four hours but have settled in already."

Zac nodded. "Yeah, we have and it's great and the village even has shops and things."

"Oh, Zac, just look at you," said Hetty, lovingly stroking his hair, "and how you've grown. I reckon you're going to be as tall as your dad."

"And his granddad," said Lottie, with pride. "Hugh was tall and I must say Zac looks very much like he did when I first met him." She sighed. "Oh, how he would have loved to be part of this holiday."

Bill and Zac put the ladies' luggage into the Volvo and then they all climbed into the car and headed towards Pentrillick.

"So, what have you been doing today?" Lottie asked from the back of the car where she sat beside Hetty.

Bill looked at his mother in the rear view mirror. "Being thoroughly lazy, I'm ashamed to say. I didn't get up until ten this morning."

"And after breakfast we went exploring," Zac added.

"Yes, Zac and I have had a good look round. Pentrillick is a lovely village and the beach is quite superb. In fact, that's where

17

Sandra and the girls have gone today, to the beach, although they're probably home by now because they said they'd be back in time for your arrival."

Hetty laughed. "You must have settled in if you're calling the cottage home."

"Good point," said Bill, "but it really is home from home."

"What's the name of the cottage?" Lottie asked. "I'm sure I've been told but I can't remember."

"It's actually called Sea View," said Bill, "although we've named it the chocolate box because it's really quaint and the gardens are breath-taking."

"Unusual for a holiday cottage," said Hetty. "Having a nice garden, that is. I wonder who looks after it."

"We wondered that," said Bill. "If we have any problems we have to contact a rather stunning lady called Rosie Rutherford who is an artist, but I shouldn't think she cleans the place or looks after the garden either. She's a bit posh, you see, so I should imagine she doesn't even do her own cleaning."

Hetty frowned. "What sort of artist is she?"

"She does paintings apparently. We saw one of her works at a café we visited in Exeter yesterday on our way down here. We've looked at her website too and her work is very well liked and she has a good name."

"And there's one of her paintings in the cottage too," said Zac, "of that place over there." He pointed back to St. Michael's Mount just visible through the trees.

"I see," said Lottie, "so do you still draw, Zac? I remember you were very talented as a child and I still have some of your little pictures."

Zac felt his face flush. "Thanks, Grandma. I do sketch a bit but seldom paint. It's easier to go out with just a sketch pad and pencils than it is with paints, easel and so forth."

"Well, there's certainly plenty of scope for painting, drawing or whatever around here," said Hetty, as the car turned down a lane and the sea sparkled on the horizon, "plenty of scope indeed."

Sandra, Vicky and Kate were back from the beach and out in the cottage garden sitting on benches around a picnic table when they heard Bill parking the Volvo. Sandra, keen to welcome the new arrivals, went indoors to greet them. After hugs and kisses she took Hetty and Lottie upstairs to show them their room on the back of the cottage with a far-reaching views out to sea.

"I'll leave you to get settled in," said Sandra, "and then when you're ready I'll put the kettle on for tea."

Thank you," said the sisters together.

"Bagsy the bed in the corner," said Hetty, hastily flinging her handbag onto the floral duvet cover as Sandra left the room.

"By all means," said Lottie, "I should prefer to be by the window anyway. It'll be lovely to look out at the sea when I wake up in the mornings. In fact I shall sleep with the window open so that I can hear the sea. I hope you don't mind, Het."

"Humph, well you mustn't leave it open when the light is on. We don't want the room full of moths." She shuddered. "I can't abide moths."

Lottie smiled. "You've never grown out of that phobia then. I remember you used to go crazy if a moth or a daddy-longlegs got in our room when we were young."

"Yes...well...I do still have a fear of moths but I'm okay with the daddy long-legs now, in fact I've even been known to catch them and put them outside."

"How about spiders?"

"No problem there. I suppose when you live alone you have to be able to deal with these things."

Lottie nodded. "Yes, living alone is something I'm still trying to come to terms with and it's not easy."

"Time will help, I'm sure," said Hetty, "and I daresay after three weeks of being surrounded by six other people you'll be glad to get back to the peace and quiet."

By early evening, the sun was no longer shining: the sky was overcast but at least it felt warm. Hetty and Lottie, keen to stretch their legs after hours spent sitting on trains, decided to take a stroll down to the beach by way of the path and steps which lay beyond the gate at the foot of the cottage garden.

At the bottom of the short flight of steps was a large cobbled area where a few boats lay alongside sandwich boards advertising fishing trips. Nearby, a small shop sold ice creams, teas, coffees and cold drinks, beach balls, buckets and spades, and anything else that might be needed for a day on the beach. On the inside of the half-glazed door hung a *closed* sign and a list of the shop's opening hours.

Further down and away from the cobbles, the beach lay nestled between the cliffs and stretched out to the left and the right. A series of tall iron posts ran from one end of the beach to the other and between them hung colourful bunting which gently flapped in the early evening breeze.

Keen to get near to the waves, Lottie and Hetty stepped onto the sand and as they walked down to the sea they passed between two benches firmly attached to concrete plinths. Once by the water's edge they gathered pebbles, threw them into the tumbling waves and laughed like children when they were forced to make a hasty retreat as the water gushed towards their stumbling feet.

Walking further along the beach, they observed a wide alleyway which they assumed led up to the village's main street. Keen to explore they took a look and found it came out between a fish and chip shop and a post office.

As they retraced their steps, Hetty and Lottie sat down on one of the benches.

"I hope those sea walls don't suffer from erosion, Het," said Lottie looking back at the chocolate box cottage and the rocks where the steps were embedded, "otherwise we might wake up in the sea one morning."

Hetty chuckled, amused at the thought. "I agree, but I think it looks solid enough and it's actually quite a distance from the sea."

Lottie nodded. "Yes, but the distance between the wall and the sea might be because it's low water now and being strangers we've no idea just how far the sea usually comes up the beach. You know, during high tide."

"Good point," said Hetty, looking over her shoulder for any indication as to a high water mark, "but I shouldn't think the sea goes up anywhere near the cobbles otherwise that shop and the boats would be in serious trouble. Although I daresay the shop closes in the winter anyway and all stock is removed to be on the safe side. I'm thinking of high winds, winter storms, wild seas and so forth."

Lottie shuddered. "Ugh, don't mention of winter. I hate the thought of it getting dark early. Come on, we must be positive, Het, and enjoy the summer while it's still here."

A sudden gust of wind whipped across the beach causing one of the sandwich boards to topple over. Feeling chilly, Hetty buttoned up her cardigan. "You're right, Lottie, and this really is a glorious spot."

"Paradise, Het."

A puzzled look crossed Hetty's face. "It just suddenly struck me. I mean, thinking about it, it doesn't seem possible that a murder took place here."

Lottie frowned. "Did you have to mention that? It's even more depressing than thinking about winter and probably best forgotten while we're here."

"Maybe, but I'm sure Faith what-ever-her-name was wouldn't want it forgotten. At least not until someone has been brought to justice."

"Faith Trethewy," said Lottie, her shoulders slumped, "that was the poor soul's name."

"That's right, I remember now." Hetty turned and looked back at the houses along the street. "I wonder where she lived. Or more to the point, I wonder where her murderer lives."

Fear shone in Lottie's eyes as they darted towards the chocolate box cottage. "Not near to us, I pray."

Chapter Four

Lottie was woken early on Monday morning by the sun shining across her pillow. She sat up and looked from the window. The morning was fine but the large clusters of clouds scuttling across the sky told her there was a fresh north-westerly wind blowing.

Lottie was familiar with weather patterns. Her late husband, Hugh, had been a keen gardener and very much the outdoor type, hence he had kept an eye on the weather throughout their married life. And still, eleven months after his passing Lottie avidly watched the weather forecast several times a day out of habit.

Leaving Hetty sleeping soundly in her corner, Lottie walked along the landing to the bathroom hoping it was free. It was and so she took a quick shower and then went downstairs to see if anyone else was up. No-one was and so she made a mug of tea and took it into the conservatory already warmed by the morning sun.

When she returned her empty mug to the kitchen she laid up the table for breakfast and then patiently waited for the rest of the family to join her. One by one the family rose from their beds and went downstairs where during breakfast they discussed how each intended to spend their day.

It was mid-morning before anyone ventured out and the first to do so was Zac having decided to take a walk along the coastal path with his sketchpad.

The cliff path, Zac found, was exposed to the elements and so he was glad he had taken his grandmother's advice and worn a jacket, for the wind was cold and mitigated any warmth radiated by the sun.

On reaching the far side of the cliff where rocks edged Pentrillick's beach, he observed a small building below the cliff face with a slipway running into the sea. A rough track, cut into the granite, led down to the building which he assumed was a lifeboat house. But he was puzzled. It seemed odd that a lifeboat house should be surrounded with tubs of flowers and decked with colourful hanging baskets.

He sat down on a patch of grass and folded back the cover of his sketchpad. As he outlined the view of the rugged coast, a couple walked close behind him and paused. To Zac's surprise, one of the couple told the other that the old lifeboat house was now the studio of Rosie Rutherford, the artist. As they walked away, Zac took his phone from the pocket of his jeans. If Rosie Rutherford was a celebrity, albeit of the art world, then he must take some pictures of her studio. When he raised his phone to do so he was delighted to see that she was actually outside the building talking to someone and so he took several. Not that he thought his pictures would impress anyone back home. After all, he'd never heard of Rosie Rutherford before their planned holiday in Cornwall and so it was unlikely that any of his friends would have either.

That same morning, Hetty and Lottie explored the village. They optimistically bought sunhats from a gift shop and then called into a charity shop for a browse around. The shop was manned by two ladies of a similar ages to the twins. According to their name badges, one was called Maisie and the other, Daisy. Hetty bought a pair of slippers because she had forgotten to pack hers and Lottie bought a couple of paperback novels.

"And are you ladies on holiday?" asked Maisie, the taller of the two assistants as she took their money.

"Yes, we are," said Hetty, "We're staying at Sea View Cottage and very nice it is too."

"So I've heard but I've not been inside. Well, not since it was done up anyway."

"You're very brave to have come down with all the kerfuffle there is over the murder of poor Faith Trethewy," said Daisy, the other assistant. "I assume you'll have heard about that."

Hetty nodded. "Yes, in fact we were only talking about it yesterday, weren't we, Lottie?"

"Yes, we were." Lottie placed the books inside her handbag.

Hetty was eager to hear more. "So do you think it has affected the holiday trade here then?" she asked.

"Oh definitely," said Daisy, obviously willing to chat, "at least it has here in Pentrillick. I know of several places that have had cancellations including the Hotel."

"Oh dear, but I can understand it," said Hetty. "My nephew looked on the Internet this morning to see if there had been any new developments but he drew a blank as it appeared there had been none at all."

"Yes, well as far as we know the police are getting nowhere fast," scoffed Daisy. "There certainly haven't been any arrests and I don't think anyone has even been 'helping with enquiries' as they like to put it."

"Oh dear, that's not very encouraging," said Lottie, clearly alarmed, "So does anyone know what the motive was? I know a phone and laptop were taken but I believe that was all."

Maisie shook her head. "You're right and that's what's so un-nerving. You see, we reckon the real reason wasn't burglary at all simply because Faith was at home, and although as you say, her laptop and phone were taken, nothing else was, but I really can't see that her murder was premeditated because well, things like that don't happen to ordinary people, do they? None of it makes sense."

"Actually," said a female customer who was browsing through a rack of summer dresses, "I've heard that it might have been an attempted burglary, after all. Faith's car *wasn't* on the driveway, you see, because it was at the garage for its MOT so it would've looked as though she'd gone out." The shopper furtively looked over her shoulder. "I heard this from Tess. You know, Tess Dobson who does a bit of cleaning for Rosie Rutherford."

The two assistants nodded. "Oh, yes, we know Tess," said Maisie, "but what makes her say it might possibly have been burglary?"

Maisie, Daisy, Hetty, Lottie and the shopper all moved closer together. "Well, keep this to yourselves," whispered the shopper, "but apparently Tess was over at Rosie's yesterday doing some ironing in the kitchen when two coppers called. Rosie was really surprised but she took them into the living room and shut the door. Needless to say Tess was curious as to what they wanted and so she crept down the hallway and listened outside the door."

"Good heavens," said Maisie, eyes like saucers, "this is news to me. So did she hear anything?"

The shopper nodded. "Oh yes, you bet she did. You see, one day last week, old Mrs Trethewy, Faith's mum, was in the cottage sorting out Faith's clothes so she could bring the good stuff down here for you ladies to sell, and you'll never guess what she found in the bottom of Faith's knicker drawer."

The ladies all shook their heads

"The mind boggles," said Daisy.

"And so it should." The shopper paused for dramatic effect. "She found money. A considerable amount of money. Twenty pound notes all in bundles and bound up with elastic bands. Mrs Trethewy was so shocked she called the police straight away. She couldn't think where her daughter could have got the money from, you see, as she only had a modest income to live on."

"So how much do you reckon there was?" Hetty asked.

"Well, according to Tess, the sum of twenty thousand pounds was mentioned. The police feel it's a break-through because now they know someone might have had a motive. They reckon someone knew about it, you see, and thought they'd nick it while Faith was out, but of course she wasn't out. Poor soul."

"Phew! Twenty thousand pounds in cash," said Maisie. "Wherever would she have got that from?"

"Well, that's what the police were hoping Rosie might be able to tell them, her being friends with Faith as well as her next door neighbour, but Rosie was as miffed as the police and everyone else I've told is completely dumbfounded as well."

Lottie scowled. "How come the police didn't find the money earlier? I mean, surely they searched the place for clues."

The shopper nodded. "That's what my old man said when I told him, but I reckon because there were no signs of it being a robbery and because Faith's handbag and purse were untouched on the sideboard, they dismissed the possibility of it being a burglary gone wrong."

"Yet her laptop and phone were both stolen," said Maisie.

"The shopper nodded. "Ah, yes, but that's another thing that's baffling me. I mean, why were they stolen? According to Rosie, Faith's phone wasn't even a smart phone and her laptop was as old as the hills. So neither were worth anything. And for that reason I reckon the police think they were both stolen just to make it look like robbery, if you see what I mean, but of course now the money's turned up it alters everything."

Daisy tutted. "Oh dear, what a puzzle. I find it very hard to retain all the facts and now you've told us about the money, it's even more confusing."

"But I still would have thought the police would have searched through all of Faith's things," persisted Lottie, who was very meticulous. "Had they done so the money would have been discovered a lot earlier."

The shopper nodded. "Yes, but Faith's clothes were all upstairs so I doubt the coppers would have suspected the killer had even been up there. No doubt they took a quick look but if nothing appeared to be disturbed then I can understand why they wouldn't have been very thorough."

"Hmm," said Hetty, "so it seems the big question is, where did Faith get the money from and who knew about it?"

The two shop assistants looked at each other. "Humph! Well, if I were the police I'd question that bloke she used to live with," said Daisy, emphatically folding her arms. "I wouldn't be surprised if Faith were looking after the money for him. I always thought he seemed a dodgy so-and-so."

The shopper shook her head. "No, I shouldn't think so, he cleared off donkey's years ago, well before that dreadful car crash."

"Dreadful car crash," repeated Hetty, keen to know every little detail.

"Yes, poor Faith was badly injured in an accident near the Marazion roundabout," said Maisie. "It must be umm…about four years ago, I'd say. She made quite a good recovery but suffered terribly with back problems afterwards. She gave up her job because of it."

"Yes, poor soul, she loved that job," said the shopper.

"Where did she work?" Lottie asked.

"Pentrillick House," said Maisie, glancing towards the door as it opened, "she was the estate manager."

As a family came into the shop, the ladies all tried to act casually.

"Pentrillick House. I recall our Bill saying something about that," said Lottie, casually picking up a vase and pretending to examine it. "Would I be right in thinking it's open to the public?"

"Yes, that's right, it's open five days a week in the winter and all seven in the summer," said Daisy, producing a leaflet. "If you drive on out of the village you'll see a turning off to the right signposted Little Trenwyn. It's up there on the left. You can't miss it."

Lottie returned the vase to the shelf and took the leaflet. "Excellent, we might have to pop up there one day then."

"Yes, it's well worth a visit. They have a garden shop and a gift shop; tea rooms too and they do excellent cream teas with local clotted cream. It's all beautifully maintained and has been used as a location for a feature film."

"Really, that's definitely one for our 'to do' list," said Hetty, hoping the family browsing through swimwear might leave so that they could find out more about Faith's murder. "I love large old houses and I should imagine the gardens are quite impressive if they have a garden shop."

"Oh, they are. There's a maze too which is quite an attraction on its own. Young Barry works up there and Louise is always saying how much he loves his job."

"Barry, Louise, who are they?" Hetty asked, beginning to feel her mind was on overload.

"Louise works in the café just down the road and Barry is her son. They both live in an ex Council house which they bought just before John, her husband died. God rest his soul."

"Oh, I see, so Louise is a widow, said Hetty, a look of disappointment on her face as even more people entered the shop.

The sisters were glad to sit down when they arrived back at the cottage. Their heads were spinning with facts, suppositions and the names of people they had never met.

Sandra, who had also just arrived back at the cottage, having spent the morning on the beach with her daughters, Vicky and Kate, was about to make a pot of tea. "So, have you ladies had a good morning?" she asked as she filled the kettle.

"Oh yes, we most certainly have," said Hetty, slipping off her shoes and trying on her newly purchased slippers, "we've been chatting to some ladies in the charity shop and we've found out a few bits of information about the poor soul who was murdered."

"As well as motives and so forth," Lottie added.

Vicky and Kate both looked up from their mobile phones.

Sandra sighed. "Oh dear, I hope it's nothing gruesome."

"No, no," said Hetty, "but it's very intriguing and I'd like to find out more. It's a real can of worms."

"Really?" said Vicky, tucking her phone into the pocket of her jeans, "Come on, Great Auntie Hetty, "tell us some of the latest details."

Hetty smiled, delighted to have the attention of her great nieces. "Very well, Kate, but for the sake of brevity I think you can drop the great and just call me Auntie Hetty."

The young twins both giggled. "Okay, Auntie Hetty, but I'm not Kate, I'm Vicky."

"The family thought about going to the Crown and Anchor for dinner in the evening but most admitted they were feeling tired and put that down to the sea air. And when Vicky said that Tom Daley and his partner Dan Goodfellow were diving at the Olympic Games around eight o'clock they all agreed to stay at the cottage instead and watch television.

To save Sandra the hassle of cooking, Bill and Zac drove down to Long Rock and bought pizzas, wine, a case of beer, and cans of Coke for the children.

Hetty wasn't really into sport and so read while the rest of the family watched the Olympics and to their delight, Tom and Dan won a bronze medal. The fourth medal for Team GB.

Chapter Five

On Tuesday morning, Sandra and Bill took the children to visit a theme park in Helston and so Hetty and Lottie with the day to themselves, decided to call at the café for coffee and to introduce themselves to Louise, if she was working, of whom the ladies in the charity shop had spoken.

They found the café on the end of a terrace of shops and houses. It was painted an attractive pale lemon colour and had standard fuchsias in tubs on either side of the door. As they crossed the threshold, a tune from the nineteen sixties greeted them and both sisters automatically swayed in time with the music as they stepped inside and took in the décor of the brightly lit room.

The dining area was rectangular in shape with sashed windows and floral curtains to the front and back. The walls were painted daffodil yellow and the floor tiles were slate grey. Seating comprised eight square tables, equidistantly spaced and on the right-hand side of the room was the counter, behind which, a middle aged woman was arranging cakes on a tray; as the door closed she promptly looked up and smiled. Wondering if she might be Louise, the sisters crossed the tiled floor towards her and asked for two coffees and two toasted teacakes. Hetty and Lottie then sat at a table near to the window which looked out over the beach where they observed the tide was in further than the previous evening.

The person they assumed to be Louise made the coffee and the order for teacakes went out to a room behind the counter where female voices could be heard chattering. When their mugs of coffee arrived, Hetty introduced herself and Lottie. To her delight, the courtesy was returned and the lady was indeed Louise. As she placed a bowl with assorted sugar sachets on their table, another person appeared from the kitchen.

"Hetty, Lottie, meet Chloe," said Louise, standing aside, "my boss and a trusted friend."

Chloe was in her mid-thirties and had rich auburn hair. She smiled sweetly as she placed the toasted teacakes on the table. "I'm pleased to meet you. Would I be right in assuming you're here on holiday?"

"Yes, and we're very much enjoying our stay," said Lottie. "And I must say I'm very impressed with your choice of colour in here: the curtains are really snazzy."

"Thank you. I come from a long line of keen gardeners so I had to have floral curtains."

"Good for you," said Lottie, "it makes a nice change as so many people go for plain these days."

"So, how long are you here for?" Chloe asked.

"Three weeks," said Lottie, "and we only arrived yesterday so we've ages yet."

"Lovely, and it seems you've brought the sunshine with you."

"The sun always shines on the righteous," laughed Hetty.

"And the unrighteous," added Lottie, quick to correct her sister.

On her way back to the kitchen, Chloe stopped to clear the table of a family who were leaving and Louise resumed her position behind the counter. As the last family member to leave closed the door, Hetty asked Louise if she recommended a visit to Pentrillick House.

"Oh, yes. It's a lovely place. A beautiful location and there's plenty to see and do while you're there. They even have their own bakery and do a delivery round to people in the village."

"Do they make these delicious teacakes?" Lottie asked, holding up the remains of her bun.

"Absolutely. Chloe buys all her bread from them and says she wouldn't dream of getting it from anywhere else."

"How refreshing to hear that," said Hetty, wistfully, "having the baker call, I mean. It stirs up all sorts of memories. Lots of things were delivered when we were nippers, weren't they, Lottie?"

Lottie nodded. "Which rather shows our age."

"My Barry works up there and does deliveries, but not bread. He works in the gardens, you see, and so with him it's plants. The house is a godsend as it provides a lot of employment for locals."

"I see," said Hetty, trying to visualise Pentrillick House and its grounds, "and we hear the poor lady who was murdered was the estate manager there."

Louise sighed. "Yes, and it was my son's friend, Kyle, who delivers the bread when he's home from university, that went to the aid of Rosie on the morning that Faith died. Fair shook the poor chap up, so I'm told."

"Oh dear, yes, it must have," Hetty agreed. "What a horrible experience for the young lad. So what exactly happened?"

Louise left her position behind the counter and went to their table so that she could be heard above the music. "Well, according to, Barry, my son, Kyle parked outside Faith's house as usual, took her order from the back of the van and as he went through her gates he heard someone scream. He dashed indoors and found Rosie in the living room kneeling beside Faith's body, sobbing. He said she were in a right state."

"So was it Rosie who screamed?" Lottie asked.

"That's right. She screamed when she found her and who could blame her." Louise shuddered. "It gives me the creeps just thinking about it."

"So how did Rosie know that Faith was in trouble?" Hetty asked, clearly puzzled.

"Apparently, she was in her driveway pulling up a few weeds when she heard sudden raised voices. She didn't think anything of it and wasn't even sure which house they were coming from, but then suddenly there were three loud bangs. At first she thought it was probably a car back firing but then she realised the shouting had stopped and she was alarmed, said she felt in her bones that something was wrong, horribly wrong and so she went next door to see if Faith had heard it. She found poor Faith on the living room floor as dead as a dodo."

"Good heavens! Poor Rosie," said Lottie.

"So did either Rosie or Kyle see anything of the murderer?" Hetty asked. "I mean, he couldn't have been far away if it'd only just happened."

Louise shook her head. "Regrettably no, but Rosie said she heard the back door of Faith's cottage slam shut at the same time as she found her. She ran into the kitchen and looked out into the back garden but there was no sign of anyone. There are a lot of trees in the field behind the houses so he would have had plenty of places to hide."

"What about the murder weapon," asked Hetty, "was it ever found?"

"Sadly not, so it's assumed the murderer took it with him. Which makes sense. I mean, he's hardly likely to leave it behind, is he?"

Hetty sighed. "No, I suppose not."

"Last question," said Lottie, realising they must sound very nosy, "where exactly are Faith and Rosie's houses?"

Louise laughed. "Quite a distance from you, you'll be pleased to know. They're up at Blackberry Way which is at the end of Long Lane."

"Oh," said Lottie, clearly none the wiser.

"Which is where?" Hetty asked, keen to know the exact location.

Louise waved he hand towards the door. "Go along the main road here until you get to the Crown and Anchor. Long Lane is opposite the pub. As the name suggests it's quite long and it's uphill too. Eventually it reaches a dirt track leading into fields. Blackberry Way is off to the right just before Long Lane ends. You can't miss it. Rosie lives in the first house, it's called Tuzzy-Muzzy and poor Faith lives, or rather lived, in Primrose Cottage which is situated next to the gates of Rosie's driveway."

"Driveway?" said Hetty. "I take it Rosie's house is somewhat larger than Faith's cottage then."

Louise nodded. "Yes it is, considerably so. It's on a corner and the gardens are huge. About an acre, so I believe. The driveway is quite short though and most of her garden is along one side and round the back."

Lottie frowned. "And what did you say Rosie's house was called?"

"Tuzzy-Muzzy. Lovely, isn't it?"

"Well, it's certainly unusual," Lottie agreed. "Any idea what it means?"

Louise nodded. "Yes, it can mean either a posy of flowers or the burrs of the burdock plant. Take your pick."

"Fascinating," said Lottie, "we must have a stroll up there one day and take a look."

The door opened and a family of four walked into the café. "I must go," said Louise. "It'll soon be lunchtime and we'll be really busy then. I hope the sun keeps shining for you." She laughed. "Well, actually for all of us."

She then left and went to greet the family.

After leaving the café the sisters walked down to the beach and sat on the same bench as on Sunday evening.

"It's surprisingly warm down here," said Hetty, glancing at the people gathered on the sand, "I thought it might be quite chilly."

"That's because it's sheltered from the north-westerly wind," said Lottie, watching the clouds drifting through the sky.

"Yes, I suppose so. Were it a lot warmer I think I might have been tempted into the sea for a paddle."

"Really?" said Lottie, "you won't catch me in there. The water's always far too cold."

"But it would be so invigorating," said Hetty, "which is good for the circulation and all that."

Lottie scowled. "If you say so. Anyway, what shall we do now? We can't sit here all day and it'd be silly to go back to the cottage so soon."

"Well I suppose we could catch a bus to Penzance. I rather liked the look of the place and if we did I could use my Senior Citizen's bus pass."

Lottie looked surprised. "I didn't know you had one. I mean, with you being a driver."

"Well, I wasn't going to bother but then Sally, one of my old work mates, said I should, after all I do live near to a bus stop. To my surprise I often use it and if the truth be known I've never been over fond of driving anyway. I really enjoy a bus ride and you can see so much more especially upstairs. You should get one, Lottie."

Lottie half-smiled. "After Hugh died Bill insisted that I got one to enable me to get out and about. I sometimes wish I'd learned to drive but I think if I had it would have been wasted. After all Hugh liked driving and very good at it he was too."

"Very sensible of you. So do you have your bus pass with you?"

Lottie nodded. "Yes, it's always in my purse."

Hetty stood up. "Then let's go to Penzance and we can have lunch there."

Lottie looked doubtful. "But can we use them down here?"

"Yes, they're valid anywhere in England and even if they weren't we could always pay. I doubt it would break the bank."

Hetty looked up the bus times on her phone and found they had only ten minutes to wait and so they walked back to the road to look for the bus stop. They knew there was one opposite the cottage but that would be for eastbound buses and so they walked along the street assuming a westbound bus stop must be nearby. They were correct in their assumption. The bus stop was outside the post office. It had no shelter but there was a bench to sit on. The bus was on time and so they hopped on board and took seats upstairs at the front.

In Marazion the bus stopped outside a pub. On seeing St. Michael's Mount from the window, Hetty promptly grabbed Lottie by the arm. "Quick, let's get off here because I'm sure that if we do we'll be able to walk along the beach to Penzance. If not we'll have a look round and then catch the next bus."

Hetty was correct in her assumption. A coastal path ran from Marazion to Penzance and to aid their journey they bought ice creams. The walk was rather exposed to the elements but in spite of the wind, the sisters enjoyed the change of scenery. Their route took them over sand dunes where sea holly and wild cabbage plants with pale yellow flowers stood tall and erect. They crossed over a stream and finally onto a path which ran alongside the main line railway track and the beach, - a long expanse of golden sand, which stretched between the footpath and the sea.

Chapter Six

Wednesday started off bright and sunny but as the weather forecast had predicted grey clouds soon rolled in and the day was marred by patchy light rain.

"Ideal day for the cinema, I think," said Sandra, ever the optimist, "what was it you girls said you wanted to see?"

"The BFG," said Kate, already searching her phone for details of the nearest cinema showing it.

Vicky looked over her sister's shoulder. "Brilliant, it's on in Penzance at one twenty five. So can we go please, Mum?"

"I'm up for it," said Sandra, "how about the rest of you?"

Zac shook his head. "Not my scene."

"What's the BFG when it's at home?" Lottie asked.

Vicky giggled. "It's the big friendly giant, Grandma. You must have heard of it. It was written by Roald Dahl donkey's years ago."

"Nineteen eighty two," said Kate, checking details on Wikipedia.

"Oh I see, yes, I've heard of Roald Dahl but I think I'll give it a miss. Your dad might like it though because if I remember correctly he read lots of Dahl's books when he was young."

Bill nodded. "Yes, I did but the fondness of back then is not enough for me to want to see the film all these years later."

Sandra looked at her husband. "Right, so you and Zac can stay here with Gran and I'll take the girls to the cinema. How about you, Auntie Hetty?"

"I'm a sucker for kid's films so I'll go with you if that's alright."

"Yes, that's fine. The more the merrier."

Bill rubbed his hands together. "Excellent, and since you'll be away at lunchtime, I shall take Mum and Zac to the pub for a bite to eat. Can't believe I've been here nearly four days and haven't set foot in the place yet."

The Crown and Anchor was built of granite; it dated back to the seventeenth century and had been a hostelry for its entire life. Situated at the opposite end of the village from Sea View Cottage, it was run by Alison and Ashley Rowe who had been the licensees for just over four years and both were on duty when Bill, Lottie and Zac arrived for lunch.

The pub was busy and so while Bill went to the bar and ordered drinks, Lottie and Zac looked for an empty table. They managed to find one near to a large potted palm beside French doors which led out onto a sun terrace, deserted due to the drizzle.

As Bill waited for his drinks he glanced along the bar; several men leaned on the counter, each perched on stools with pint glasses in hands. Bill listened, judging by the subject of their conversation - the money stashed away in Faith Trethewy's knicker drawer - he concluded all were locals. Most were white haired and he assumed retired, but one, whose age it was impossible to judge because his features were hidden behind a thick bushy beard, dark glasses and the peak of a dark blue cap, spoke of his need to get back to work.

As Bill sat down with the family and handed them their drinks, the bearded stranger banged his empty glass on the bar, wiped his mouth on the back of his hand and bade his colleagues farewell. Ashley turned away from the till when he heard the door open. "Bye Bernie," he called, "see you tomorrow."

Bernie nodded as he closed the door.

"Who was that scruffy looking oik?" said Lottie, without thinking.

"No idea," said Bill, "unless he was a fisherman."

Zac shook his head. "Can't be, Dad. At least if he is he's not from here because there are never any fishing boats amongst the vessels on the beach."

"Good point," said Bill, as he picked up the menu lying on the table, "have you two decided what you'd like to eat?"

"A ham sandwich will do me fine," said Lottie, "preferably with wholemeal bread."

"Cheeseburger and chips for me," said Zac, "I'm starving."

"And I'll have the same," said Bill closing up the menu, "but don't tell your mother or she'll nag. Too many calories and all that."

Lottie tutted. "And she'd be more than justified, Bill. It's alright for Zac because he's a growing lad, but you…well…you've grown enough."

By evening the rain had passed, the sky was looking brighter and so Sandra feeling in need of fresh air and exercise, suggested they all take a walk after they had eaten dinner. To her surprise, everyone agreed and so all seven strolled through the village and then out along the lane down which they had driven when they had first arrived on Saturday. As they turned a corner, a signpost pointed off to the right and on it was the name Little Trenwyn.

"Ah, now that must be the lane that leads to Pentrillick House where poor Faith Trethewy worked as estate manager," said Hetty, delighted to have come across it. "We'll be able to go there now that we've tracked it down."

It was dusk when they arrived back at the cottage and although no-one was tactless enough to mention it, everyone had been conscious as the skies had darkened that there may well be a murderer in their midst. Hence all were very glad to get back inside behind locked doors with the curtains drawn.

However, thoughts of Faith's demise remained with Sandra as she sat down in the sitting room with a glass of wine and so to satisfy her curiosity, she opened up her laptop and logged onto Facebook. Without saying a word to rest of the family she typed Faith Trethewy in the search box. To her surprise she found her name easily and knew she had the correct Faith for there was mention of Pentrillick House.

Sandra clicked onto Faith's profile. She sighed. Such a pretty woman. Blonde with lovely blue eyes. With a lump in her throat she scrolled down Faith's Timeline where endless messages of condolence followed one after another. And all shared the same sentiments…that Faith would be missed, was much liked and was a great loss to Pentrillick. Sandra shuddered, unnerved by the sudden thought that the killer himself may have left false sentiments amongst the numerous messages.

"Mum, why are you frowning?" Kate asked.

"What! No, no I wasn't."

Kate was adamant. "You were." Keen to see what her mother was looking at, she jumped up and looked over Sandra's shoulder. "Oh, you're checking out the poor dead woman. That's not nice."

Hetty sat bolt upright. "What's that?"

"Mum's found the murdered woman on Facebook."

"What Faith Trethewy?" Hetty sprang to her feet. "Well done, Sandra. It never occurred to me to look on Facebook for her. Are there any useful clues on her Timeline?"

Bill tutted. "I hardly think anyone would be that daft."

"You never know," said Hetty, "some people are very careless. Read out the names of her friends, Sandra."

Sandra frowned. "What all two hundred and twenty four of them?"

Lottie gasped. "Faith had two hundred and twenty four friends? But that's amazing."

Kate giggled. "Facebook friends aren't like real friends, Grandma, they're just acquaintances. You know, like people from school and stuff like that."

Lottie frowned. "School…stuff…but…"

"Never mind, Lottie," interrupted Hetty, "I'll explain later. Now Sandra, please read out the names because I'm really interested to see how many we'll recognise."

Bill laughed. "But we've only been here for five days and you've only been here for four. You'll know less than a dozen."

"Pessimist," said Hetty. But much to her annoyance, Bill was right.

"Oh well, it was worth a try," she said, sitting back down on the settee, "and at least we know we have somewhere where we can go to investigate people's characters as we get to know them. You know what I mean. If we come across anyone behaving suspiciously we can check them out on Facebook to see if they were Faith's friends and so forth."

Bill tutted. "My dear, Aunt Hetty, I can assure you that the police will have been through the list of Faith's friends with a fine tooth comb, so I really think you'd be wasting your time."

"Don't be such a killjoy, Bill," said Lottie, wishing she understood all that her sister had said.

"Well, who knows? You may be right, Bill," said Hetty, sweetly, "but the police didn't bother looking in Faith's knicker drawer, did they? So they may not have checked her Facebook friends either."

Chapter Seven

"Grandma and I are thinking of going to visit Pentrillick House today now that we know how to get there," said Hetty during breakfast on Thursday morning, "would anyone like to join us?"

Vicky sighed. "Oh dear, I'd say yes because I'd like to see how long it would take me to get out of the maze there, but Kate and me thought we'd go swimming today as the weather is looking promising."

"Kate and I," corrected her grandmother, looking over the top of her spectacles.

Hetty suppressed a smile. Vicky gritted her teeth. "Sorry. Kate and I," she hissed.

"How do you know there's a maze?" Sandra asked, as she tipped natural yoghourt onto her muesli.

"Because I picked up a Pentrillick House leaflet at the ice cream stall on the beach the other day and there's a picture of it with people inside. The hedges look really high."

"Oh, I see," said Sandra, "I must admit that does sound interesting and I've never seen a maze other than in murder mystery films on television."

"How will you get there?" asked Bill, addressing his mother and aunt as he spread a thick layer of marmalade on a slice of toast, "it's a fair way to walk."

"Well, when we were poking around in the garden the other day, we discovered there are some bikes in the shed," said Hetty, with a twinkle in her eyes, "so we thought we'd take them. The tyres are pumped up and they look roadworthy."

Bill nodded. "Sounds a good idea. Nice bit of exercise if you feel up to it."

"Oh, we're up for it alright," said Hetty, with enthusiasm, "and if I remember correctly there are four bikes so would anyone else like to join us?"

Sandra bit her bottom lip. "I'd like to go but I really think I ought to go with the girls to keep an eye on them."

"Oh, come on, Mum," said Vicky, indignantly, "we're not babies anymore. We're quite capable of looking after ourselves."

"I agree," Bill said, licking marmalade from his fingers, "and they're both very good swimmers as well."

"Yes, I know, but even the best of swimmers sometimes get into trouble," Sandra persisted, "especially in the sea where there are funny tides and things like that."

"Mum, there's always a lifeguard on the beach so you really don't have to worry. Besides, there's bound to be loads of other people in the sea as well as us."

"What's more," Zac added, with a chuckle, "you can't swim, Mum, so you wouldn't be a great deal of help anyway."

Sandra laughed and raised her hands in submission. "Okay, I give in. The girls can go to the beach and I shall go with Auntie Hetty and Grandma to Pentrillick House. But I insist we take the car because I'm not safe on two wheels. Never have been due to a poor sense of balance."

"That's a relief," chuckled Bill, who had given up trying to teach his wife how to ride a bicycle many years before.

Sandra smiled to hide her embarrassment. "Yes, well, anyway, so what do you males propose to do today?"

Bill reached for another slice of toast. "I'm going to make enquiries about fishing trips. When I was in the paper shop the other morning the old dear working there told me that a chap called Bernie the Boatman goes out daily."

"And I'm going out somewhere sketching but I've not decided where yet," said Zac.

Hetty, Lottie and Sandra were enthralled by the short drive to Pentrillick House. The narrow road leading to the main entrance ran alongside one of the estate's five foot high dry stone boundary walls above which tall trees swayed in the fresh north westerly breeze creating dappled shade on the quiet country lane.

40

On arriving at the entrance they passed between two open wrought iron gates and then followed signposts along a curved track which led to a busy car park.

After looking at a notice board with opening hour details and a map of the grounds they also discovered that tours of the house took place three times a day, but as the weather was glorious they decided to remain outdoors to explore the grounds and leave a tour of the house for another day when the weather was inclement.

The three storey house was surrounded by beautifully landscaped gardens and in a valley at the foot of an avenue of trees, swans gracefully swam on the shimmering water of a large lake. Behind the house, a walled garden provided protection to flourishing rows of vegetables and on a south facing wall at the far end, two huge lean-to glasshouses, cosseted tomatoes, cucumbers, peppers, aubergines, chillies and exotic flowers.

At the garden centre they saw Barry; he was spotted by Hetty who declared it must be him for he had the same shaped nose as his mother Louise. Her surmise was confirmed once they were in close proximity of the lad by the name badge he wore beneath the estate's motif on his dark green polo shirt.

Hetty wanted to ask questions and probe into the life of Faith Trethewy, her interest in the case having heightened since hearing of the money stashed away in the knicker drawer. However, Lottie forbade her to pester the lad who was consciously working alongside an older man who was probably his superior.

After leaving the garden centre they strolled down to the lake where a wooden café lay subtly built to blend in with the surrounding woodland and a boathouse resting nearby at the water's edge.

The café provided teas, light refreshment and hot lunches and as the ladies were all feeling peckish they ordered some food and ate it outside in the shade of a magnificent silver birch tree.

"What's the name of the chappie who owns this place?" Lottie asked, as she sliced her ham baguette into small pieces. "I've forgotten."

"Tristan Liddicott-Treen," said Hetty, who had read the leaflet about Pentrillick House several times over and also looked at its website. "And if the pictures of him I've seen are a true likeness, then he's drop-dead gorgeous."

"What sort of age is he then?" Lottie asked.

"In his forties, I should imagine."

Lottie chuckled. "Hmm, for a minute I thought you might have desires on becoming the lady of the manor but if he's only in his forties he's a bit too young for you."

Hetty shrugged her shoulders, "Well, as it happens he's married anyway. I can't remember his wife's name but they have two teenage children called Jemima and Jeremy who apparently help with the running of the house during the holidays when they're home from boarding school."

Sandra cast her eyes over the landscape. "I wonder whereabouts the maze Vicky mentioned is. I haven't seen it, have either of you?"

"Good point," said Hetty, taking her mobile phone from her handbag. "I'll check it out."

She went to the Pentrillick House website and studied a plan of the grounds. "It's back there," she said, waving her hand towards the house, "behind the rose garden. Shall we go and take a look?"

Lottie wasn't too keen. "I'm not sure that I want to get lost in a maze. Not with a murderer on the loose."

Sandra looked alarmed. "Oh, I hadn't thought of that and so I think I agree."

"What a couple of wimps," said Hetty, putting away her phone.

Lottie shook her head. "No, we're just being cautious. We're here for a while yet anyway so meanwhile if the police catch the murderer then I'll be more than happy to come here again and go for a wander round the maze."

Sandra nodded. "Me too."

By the time Sandra, Hetty and Lottie arrived back at the cottage the sky had darkened and the sun was hidden behind a cluster of fast moving black clouds, hence they found both girls back from the beach and eating baked beans on toast.

"Are Dad and Zac not home yet?" Sandra asked, picking up the girls' wet swimming things from the kitchen floor.

"They've gone down to the shop," said Vicky. "Dad said his flip-flops are wearing a bit thin and he can feel all the stones on the path through them so he's gone to see if he can get a stronger pair. He tried to get some from the shop on the beach but they didn't have his size."

"I see, and did he have any luck finding out about fishing trips?"

Vicky shrugged her shoulders. "No idea but I did see him talking to an old bloke."

Bill and Zac arrived back soon after, each with a new pair of flip-flops. "We saw Rosie Rutherford in the shop," said Bill, kicking off his old flip-flops and trying on the new. "Not having seen her before in the flesh, I wasn't one hundred percent sure if it was her despite the auburn hair, but knew it was when I heard a man in the queue telling her how much he loves her work."

"And he called her Rosie," Zac added.

Bill nodded. "That's right. Anyway, when he'd gone I introduced myself and then asked her who maintained the gardens here at the cottage. Apparently it's looked after by the Pentrillick Estate, because as well as having a garden centre they also have a team of gardeners who do garden work wherever it's needed and evidently most of the work is at holiday cottages."

"Oh, so will they come while we're here?" Sandra asked.

Bill nodded. "Yes, Rosie said they will. Usually they weed, deadhead and so forth on change-over days but because we're here for three weeks they'll pay us a visit before then. They won't just turn up out of the blue though; they'll let us know when they're coming."

"Really," said Hetty, thoughts flashing through her mind, "Well, whenever they come I shall be ready and waiting with a list of questions about Faith and her activities."

"It'll probably even be Barry," said Sandra, "that's if he is part of the hire team."

"Hmm, good point, we must question Louise when next we're in the café," said Hetty, "and try and find out."

Sandra made tea for the adults which they took into the conservatory still warm in spite of the sun's absence.

"Did you manage to find the boat chappie?" Sandra asked Bill, remembering that that was the object of his morning's plans.

Bill nodded. "I did indeed." He turned to Lottie. "And I have the answer to the question you posed me yesterday, Mum. You know, about who the oik was, as you called him, who we saw in the pub.

Well, he's Bernie the Boatman and I have to admit he seems a very nice chap."

"Does he live locally?" Hetty asked.

"Yes, from what I could make out he lives in a bungalow somewhere near to the church." Bill placed his empty mug on the floor. "To my surprise I learned he's married. Silly, I know, but because he looked a little uncared for I assumed he was a crusty old bachelor but he mentioned his wife more than once."

"Been in the area long?" Hetty asked, her eyebrows raised.

Bill frowned. "No idea. Why do you ask?"

"Hmm, no reason," said Hetty, in a manner which clearly said she had a reason.

Lottie tutted." Surely you don't think he might in any way be involved in the death of poor Faith, do you, Het?"

Hetty looked sheepish. "It's a possibility," she said, "and for that reason I'm trying to catalogue the locals in my mind as we get to know them. I must admit it's quite a slow process though and it might well be time to go home before I have a list long enough to scrutinise."

"I think you watch too many detective programmes on television, Auntie Het," said Sandra, laughing as she collected the empty mugs. "I should think whoever the murderer is left the area weeks ago. I hope so anyway."

"Yes, I admit that's a possibility," said Hetty, with an impish grin, "but I shall still keep my options open and make a few enquiries. What's more, I'll keep an eye on this Bernie the Boatman if I ever get to see him. My sixth sense tells me there's more to him than meets the eye and my sixth sense is always spot on."

"Always?" queried Lottie.

"Well, sometimes."

Later that evening, the adults sat around the table in the dining room playing Scrabble, while Zac and the girls watched the television in the sitting room and cheered on Team GB who were competing in the women's gymnastics.

As Sandra used up her last letter and the game finished, she totted up the scores and declared herself the winner for the second time that evening.

"Right, who's for another game?" she asked, as the others tipped their remaining letters onto the board.

"Not sure that I want to play again," said Bill, who had scored badly, "my letters were rubbish for both games. I might go and watch the telly with the kids."

"Dear, dear," tutted Lottie, "you mustn't be a bad loser, Bill. It's only a game."

"So, shall we have another go?" Sandra asked. But before anyone had a chance to answer their attention was drawn to the whirring of a helicopter flying nearby.

"That sounds very low," said Bill, rising and crossing to the window, glad of an excuse to leave the table. He pulled back the curtain but despite the fact the cloud had gone and the night was clear it was still dark out and he could see very little. Not one to be thwarted, he went through to the conservatory and then out into the back garden. The children having also heard the helicopter, appeared from inside the sitting room and together they all followed Bill outside.

A short distance away the light of a helicopter was visible out towards the cliffs; it appeared to be hovering but it was too dark to ascertain for what purpose.

"What a racket," said Hetty, placing her hands over her ears. "The people further along the village won't be able to hear themselves think."

Kate climbed up onto a garden bench hoping that she might be able to see more. "I wonder what it's doing," she said, none the wiser for her better vantage point.

"Probably an exercise of some sort," said Lottie, feeling chilled by the cold wind as it whipped around the side of the cottage.

"Yes, I know what you mean," said Sandra, "search and rescue type stuff. I suppose they're making use of the good visibility of a clear night."

Vicky yawned. "Well, whatever, it looks pretty boring to me. I'm going back inside."

"So am I," said Hetty, "I'm sure if it's doing anything exciting we'll hear in the morning."

"Exciting?" Lottie queried. "Like what?"

Hetty shrugged her shoulders. "Like pursuing the murderer or something like that."

"Cool," said Vicky.

"I think you're being over dramatic," said Bill, amused by his aunt's determination to see justice for Faith Trethewy done, "I mean, for a start, that's not a police helicopter."

Hetty scowled. "How do you know?"

"Because it's the wrong colour," chuckled Bill.

Chapter Eight

The cold, blustery north westerly wind which had blown for the first few days of the holiday, abated on Friday morning and went round to the south west, so observed Lottie as she hung out some washing on the rotary drier. As she pegged the last item on the line she looked to the overcast skies; according to the forecast the weather should brighten up later in the day and she had every faith that it would.

Inside the family were eating breakfast, except for Zac who had popped down to the shop for more milk. When he returned his face was flushed; he placed the milk on the table and attempted to catch his breath.

"Sorry, been running," Zac panted, "and you'll never guess why." He sat down and fanned his face with a place mat.

The family all nonplussed shook their heads.

"Well, it's because there were several people in the shop and they were all talking, very loud I might add and so I couldn't help but listen. It was about the helicopter we heard last night, you see. As Dad said, it wasn't the police, it was a rescue helicopter. It wasn't an exercise though, it was actually looking for some poor chap who was missing." Zac paused momentarily to catch his breath.

"And did they find him?" Bill asked.

Zac sighed. "Yes and no. That is they did eventually find him but by then it was too late because the poor thing was already dead."

Lottie gasped. "Oh my goodness, that's awful. So what happened? Had he drowned, fallen or what?"

"I'm not sure," said Zac, putting the place mat back on the table.

Hetty saddened by the news released her grip on the spoon in her cereal bowl. "But that's dreadful and the poor rescue people, my heart bleeds for them. It must be very harrowing when their attempts are in vain."

"Was he a holiday maker, do you know?" Bill asked.

Zac shook his head. "No, apparently he was a local lad and I've got a sneaky feeling he might be the chap I've heard you talking about. He's called Barry Pascoe and he worked in the gardens up at Pentrillick House."

Lottie and Hetty both gasped simultaneously. "Barry! Yes, we knew him," said Hetty, turning pale. "That is to say, we knew of him and actually saw him at Pentrillick House only yesterday."

Lottie was too shaken to speak.

"So what exactly happened, Zac?" Bill asked, wringing his hands. "I mean, had the lad been out in a boat, fishing or what?"

Zac's face turned pale as the reality of the situation sank in. "Evidently he was just out walking with Leonard who at first I assumed was a friend but later discovered was Barry's Labrador. No-one knows yet what happened but the alarm was raised by his mum when Leonard came home alone with his lead dragging behind him. The poor dog seemed fretful and was eager for someone to follow him."

"Louise," said Hetty, tears prickling her eyes, "his mum is Louise. We've met her as she works in the cafe. Oh dear, the poor soul will be absolutely devastated. She was widowed a few years back and Barry is, or rather was, her only child."

Sandra's face was white and her body felt chilled. The thought of losing any of her children in a tragic accident or by any other means was too horrible to contemplate.

Partly through curiosity to learn more about the tragedy and partly because they were genuinely eager to convey their heart-felt sympathy to Louise, Hetty and Lottie walked down to the café mid-morning on the off-chance that it would be open. It was but as they expected, Louise was not working. Chloe, the proprietor, was just opening up assisted by two young girls.

"I can't tell you how sorry we are to have learned of the death of Louise's son," said Lottie, fighting back the tears.

"And in such a tragic way," added Hetty.

Chloe's mouth curled into a smile but her eyes, red from crying, looked sad. She was clearly upset.

"We didn't know whether you'd be open today," said Lottie, softly. "I mean, we knew Louise wouldn't be here…but…well…you know."

"I did think of not opening this morning but to be honest I can't really afford not to," said Chloe, "August is the busiest month of the year, you see and when all is said and done not opening wouldn't make things any better, would it?" Her voice croaked with emotion. "I mean, it wouldn't bring poor Barry back."

Sadly not," said Lottie. "Nothing can make a situation like this any better."

"Only time," said Hetty, "only time."

"When you next see Louise, please convey our condolences," said Lottie. "Tell her it's from the ladies staying at the chocolate box cottage."

Chloe frowned. "Yes, of course I will, but where did you say you're staying?"

"Sea View Cottage," said Hetty, casting a withering look at her sister, "but because it's so pretty the family refer to it as the chocolate box."

"Oh, oh, I see," said Chloe, as the penny dropped.

"Is it all right if we stay?" Lottie asked.

"Of course," said Chloe, "can I get you anything?"

"Yes please," said Lottie, "may we have a couple of coffees? Whenever you're ready, that is, as we've all the time in the world."

Chloe nodded. "Of course. I need to keep myself busy to take my mind off things."

The sisters sat down.

"And a couple of toasted teacakes too," said Hetty, "I didn't eat much breakfast after hearing about poor Barry and now my tummy's rumbling."

Chloe looked in the back room and asked for two tea cakes; she then went behind the counter to prepare the coffees. "So, if you're staying at Sea View Cottage would you be the competition winners? I heard some time back that Lance had donated the cottage as a prize for a holiday in August. We all assumed he thought it would be good publicity and I daresay it was because I vaguely remember hearing that it'd had a huge response."

Lottie half-smiled. "Yes, but it was actually my daughter-in-law who won the competition and she, her husband and family asked me and Hetty along too. We're sisters, twins, in fact, and Bill is my son."

"And my nephew," said Hetty.

"I see, a real family holiday then."

"Yes. So who is this Lance who owns the cottage?" Lottie asked, glad the conversation had moved away from the tragedy. "Sandra told us Rosie mentioned him when she delivered flowers on the day they arrived but apparently she didn't actually say who he was."

Chloe placed their coffees on the table. "He's the editor of the newspaper that ran the competition. He bought the cottage a few years back and stays there now and again but most of the time it's occupied by holiday makers. He and Rosie Rutherford are good friends. I don't think they knew each other before they met down here and at one time we all thought they might be romantically linked but I think it was just idle gossip and they've only ever been friends."

"So, is there a man in Rosie's life now?" Hetty was curious to know.

Chloe shrugged her shoulders. "Not that I know of. She often pops up-country though for art exhibitions and stuff like that and I believe she has a flat in London. She might have someone up there but I've never seen or heard of her having a chap down here. Having said that she has loads of friends and acquaintances. Admirers too, of course."

"That's nice. So do you live nearby, Chloe?"

"Quite near," she replied, with a gentle chuckle. She pointed to the ceiling. "I live upstairs with my hubby, Colin, in a nice little flat."

As Lottie and Hetty left the café the sun came out and so they decided to walk further along the main street towards the Crown and Anchor and from there amble along the lane which led to Blackberry Way. For both were keen to acquaint themselves with the exact location of Rosie's house and the cottage where poor Faith had lost her life.

Long Lane was all up-hill, steep in parts and narrow too. It twisted and turned and at times the sisters found it impossible to see over the tops of the tall overgrown hedges.

"If I lived here I'd seriously consider having a dog," said Hetty, pausing to break a spray of honeysuckle from the hedgerow, "I've often thought about it since I retired, you see, but always convinced myself it wouldn't really be a good idea living in the town and so forth."

"Well I never," said Lottie, stepping aside as a cyclist whizzed past heading downhill, "I've never thought of you as being a doggy person."

Hetty tucked the honeysuckle into the top button hole of her cardigan. "No, and that's because I've never been one, but I must admit the idea appeals to me now. It'd be company too and it'd make me get out of the house in the winter. But as I said, I don't think it's a good idea living in a town. Not with all the traffic on the roads."

"So if you lived out in the country what type of dog would you like?"

Hetty shrugged her shoulders. "I'm not really sure. I mean, to be honest I don't really know one breed of dog from another, apart from the obvious ones like Alsatians, Dalmatians and poodles. But it'd have to be something not too big, nor too small. It'd have to have a sweet face and not be the sort that left hair all over the place. Oh, and it mustn't bark a lot either because that would drive me mad. I'm not sure what colour I'd go for but I wouldn't have a new one. I'd get one from a rescue kind of place."

Lottie laughed. "I think you should go for it, Het, even if you do live in a town. It'd change your life and I'm sure you'd never regret it."

Hetty nodded. "Yes, well maybe I'll give it some more thought when I get home. It'd certainly make up for the family I've never had. Not since I've been grown-up, that is. I mean, I obviously had a family when I was a kid."

Towards the end of Long Lane another lane appeared on the right. "Blackberry Way, I assume," said Lottie. And as she spoke she noticed a road sign which confirmed her assumption. "I wonder if there are any blackberries along here."

"Must be," said Hetty, "or at least there must have been at one time." She sighed, "that's something else I'd do if I lived somewhere like this. I'd go blackberrying and make lots of jam."

"I used to make jam when Bill and Barbara were little," said Lottie. "I used plums from the tree in our back garden. I don't bother nowadays though because I seldom eat jam so the plums get left for the wasps. Although Sandra often takes a few when they're ripe to make a plum crumble. Apparently that's a favourite with the grandchildren. "

"Well, actually I never eat jam either but I'd still like to make some and then donate it to harvest festivals and things like that."

In all there were eight houses along Blackberry Way, all detached and no two were alike. The first one they encountered was Rosie's on the corner but the house itself wasn't visible from the road. Beyond the gates ran a winding driveway which veered off to the left and disappeared behind a collection of trees and shrubs.

Lottie studied the name on the gate. "Tuzzy-Muzzy. What was it that Louise said it meant?"

Hetty shook her head. "Can't remember exactly but it was something to do with flowers."

The next house was a modest detached cottage and clearly visible over the boundary wall. The gardens were a good size; a single garage stood away from the house and had a lean-to greenhouse on its side. Parked on the tarmac was a blue VW Beetle and on one of the closed double wooden gates was the name Primrose Cottage.

"Poor Faith," said Lottie, "and poor cottage too. It must be so lonely standing here empty and with no-one to care for it. Such a shame and I see that already the garden is starting to get quite overgrown."

Hetty frowned. "I don't think that buildings have emotions, Lottie. Which is a pity really because if they did we could ask Primrose Cottage who killed its mistress."

Lottie smiled but didn't respond. Instead she crossed the lane and leaned on a five bar gate which led into a field of wheat. At the foot of the hill the village lay neatly tucked in the valley and beyond it the deep blue sea stretched to the distant horizon. "What a beautiful spot this is, Het. The views are quite breath-taking. And look," she said, pointing ahead, "there's our chocolate box cottage."

Hetty joined her sister's side and rested her arms on top of the gate. "Yes, so it is. You know, that's something I wish I had back home. A view, I mean." She laughed. "All I can see from my garden are houses, more houses, the road and traffic."

When Hetty and Lottie arrived back at Sea View Cottage they found the adults in the back garden with Zac. The girls had gone to the beach.

"Come and sit down here," said Sandra rising from the bench, "and I'll make you both a cup of tea."

"Oh, lovely dear, that would be nice," said Hetty as they both sat down.

Bill looked quizzically at the two ladies, both red faced and puffing. "You both look a little flustered. Have you been running?"

"Cheeky," said Hetty, adjusting the cushion behind her back. "We've actually been out walking. We went up Long Lane which as the name suggests is very long and it's up-hill too. Mind you, it wasn't so bad coming back, was it, Lottie?"

Lottie shook her head. "No, it wasn't but it was still warm work."

"So what made you go up there?" Bill asked.

"We were curious to see where Rosie Rutherford lives," said Lottie.

"And where poor Faith died," Hetty added.

Bill frowned. "Wasn't that a bit morbid?"

Hetty shook her head. "No, not at all. There was nothing morbid to see and her cottage looks just like any other. In fact, you'd never suspect anything unpleasant had ever happened there. Which I suppose is just as well."

"Hmm," Bill looked unconvinced, "how about Rosie's place? What's that like?"

"Well, we couldn't actually see her house," said Lottie, because it was hidden behind trees and so forth. It's a lovely spot though with absolutely fantastic views. We could see this cottage from up there and the sea of course."

"Yes, I can imagine, and so you must be able to see the houses up there from down here."

"Good point," said Lottie, "I shall look next time I'm out the front."

"Anyway, have you two ladies worked up an appetite?" Bill asked.

The sisters looked at each other and nodded. "I rather think we have," said Hetty.

"Good, because, we've decided to go to the pub for dinner tonight around eightish. Hope you're both happy with that."

"Lovely," said Lottie, rubbing her hands together in anticipation, "there were several tempting things on the pub menu that I should like to try."

Hetty, however, frowned. "Can't we go a little bit later? I should like to see *Gardeners' World*, you see, and it's not on until half past eight."

"Oh dear, we can't go that late because they stop doing food at nine," said Bill, "Couldn't you miss it, just this week?"

Hetty looked downcast. "I never miss it. It's one of the highlights of my week. Sad I know."

"Perhaps it'll be on the telly in the pub," said Zac, trying to be helpful.

Bill shook his head. "No, I very much doubt it. If the television's on at all it'll be showing the Olympics."

Zac sighed. "Yes, of course."

"I agree but not to worry as there's quite an easy solution," said Hetty. "You all go at eight o'clock as planned and I shall stay here, have a sandwich and watch *Gardeners' World* and then when it's finished I shall join you. Problem solved."

Bill nodded. "Well if you're happy with that, then that's fine with me."

"I'm more than happy and I'm quite well acquainted with the route from here to the pub so no problem there either."

It was dusk when Hetty locked the front door of Sea View Cottage and dropped the key into her handbag. As she closed the little wooden gate, she was struck by how quiet and still the village seemed in the impending darkness. There was no traffic on the road and no-one walking along the street. The air was motionless and the ambience felt eerie almost sinister.

A truck was parked on the pavement outside the community centre blocking her way and so Hetty crossed the road and walked along the pavement there. As she passed by the church and the graveyard she quickened her pace and tried to avert her eyes from the rows of tombstones and the grotesque gargoyles staring down from the tall church tower.

A sudden feeling of unease crept into her mind as she continued through the village. Who lived in all the houses? She had no idea, but somewhere in one of them might live the person who was responsible for Faith Trethewy's death.

Hetty shuddered, looked over her shoulders and sang quietly to herself so that she felt not quite so alone. Desperate to get to the pub, her quickening pace gradually turned into a steady jog. Just before she reached the village hall, she passed a bungalow where a large dog leapt up at the gate and barked loudly. Hetty screamed, jumped in panic and quickly crossed the road as a voice from inside the bungalow told the dog to be quiet. Her jog progressed into a sprint and with heart rapidly thumping, she ran without stopping until she reached the Crown and Anchor where she stumbled in through the doorway looking very much the worse for wear.

Chapter Nine

Cloudy skies and light drizzle hampered any outdoor plans for Saturday morning but as Hetty and Lottie were not ones for the beach anyway they decided to visit the café for coffee, and leave the rest of the family to determine how best to spend their day. For both were fully aware that it wasn't right for youngsters, and teenagers in particular, to have aged relatives foisted upon them for long periods of time, especially when on holiday. To their surprise the village seemed quiet as they made their way along the main street and when they arrived at the café they found it was devoid of customers, although it had only just opened up.

"It's change over day," said Chloe, when they expressed their surprise at finding they had the café to themselves, "so it's always quiet on a Saturday morning. It'll soon be busy enough though."

The two sisters sat down. "And how is poor Louise?" Lottie asked.

"She's bearing up," said Chloe, placing small vases of flowers on each table. "I went round to see her last night and she reckons she's coming back to work on Tuesday. Personally I think it's far too soon. I mean, they've not even buried the poor lad yet, but she says she'd be far better out doing something rather than just sitting at home moping. I can see her point of view but I still don't think it's a very good idea."

Lottie sighed. "Oh dear, it must be very hard for her especially being a widow. I know what it's like to live alone; it must dreadful for her to have no-one at home to comfort her."

"Well actually she does have a gentleman friend," said Chloe, "Malcolm Biggins, he's a potter and lives in the village. You'll no doubt have seen some of his work in the gift shops around here. In fact Louise works a couple of days a week in his workshop packing up orders that have been bought on-line."

"Oh, that's good," said Lottie, genuinely pleased, "not that I recall seeing the name Malcolm Biggins, but then we haven't really looked at any pottery. It's good she has someone anyway. I'd hate to think of her going through all this alone."

"Did Faith have a boyfriend?" Hetty asked, realising that she's never thought to ask anyone before.

Chloe paused and looked over her shoulder towards the back kitchen before she answered. "Yes, quite a few but obviously not all at the same time." She lowered her voice. "I don't really like to speak ill of the dead but when it came to men she wasn't really fussy whether they were married or single, if you follow my drift and so for that reason she made quite a few enemies over the years. Having said that, as a person she was lovely. Really lovely. You know, nice temperament, happy, lively and she'd do anything for anyone."

Lottie opened her mouth to respond but was too shocked to speak.

"What about young Barry? Hetty asked. "Did he have a girlfriend?"

Chloe shook her head. "Not that I know of. Louise reckons he must have though because he used to go out most nights but then most youngsters do, don't they? If he did have a girlfriend then he never mentioned anyone to his mum."

Chloe called to one of the girls who could be heard stacking crockery in the kitchen. "Do you know if Barry had a girlfriend, Emma?"

Emma, a slim dark haired girl in her late-teens appeared in the doorway with a tea towel in her hands. She shook her head. "Not that I know of. I mean, he's been out with several of us local girls over the years, me included, but none of it was at all serious and I'm pretty sure he was unattached when he died. Unless he had a secret love somewhere, which I doubt because he wasn't a secretive person." She sighed. "Poor Baz. I can't believe he's gone and that I'll never see him again."

"How dreadful for you all," said Lottie, sympathetically. "Life is very cruel at times."

"It certainly is," Chloe agreed. "My brother and Barry were friends. They were both into gardening, you see. Poor Alfie, he's really cut up."

"Oh, I am sorry," said Lottie, "Does your brother work at Pentrillick House too?"

Chloe shook her head. "No, he works and lives in Penzance."

"Very nice too," said Lottie, "we rather like it there and love the fact it's by the sea."

"Yes, we do," said Hetty. She turned to face Emma. "So what do you youngsters like to do in your spare time?"

Emma shrugged her shoulders. "All sorts really. In the summer when we have more time we go out kayaking and of course swimming. For the rest of the year most of us are at college. I'm doing a course in Hospitality and Tourism and so during term time much of my time is taken with study." She giggled, "But we can always find time to go to the pub and play pool and several of the boys are on the Crown and Anchor team which means they need to practise all the year round. Baz was a brilliant player and thanks to him the pub was often top of the winter league. Kyle's good too but he can't play on the team because he's away at uni for most of the winter months." She sighed. "I don't think the team will do very well next season without Baz."

"I've never played pool," said Hetty. "I always think of it as a chap's game. Likewise snooker. Are you girls any good?"

"We're so so, but we could never play at match level. To us it's just a bit of fun and an evening out."

By the time Hetty and Lottie left the café the day had brightened up and the sun was out so when they arrived back at the cottage they weren't at all surprised to find the front door locked and the key under the marigold pot.

On the kitchen table was a note saying that all of the family had gone down to the beach. After a few brief words Lottie and Hetty decided to join them.

As they expected Vicky and Kate were both in the water. Zac was on the far side of the beach lying on rocks reading a joke book which he'd found in a cupboard at the cottage and Sandra sat on a blanket reading a novel.

"Someone's been busy," said Hetty, eying a huge sandcastle near to where Sandra sat, "it's most impressive."

"That was the girls," said Sandra as she moved over to make room for the sisters on the blanket, "although Bill filled up a few buckets as well."

"Where is Bill?" Lottie asked.

"Over there." Sandra nodded to where Bill stood talking to the man Lottie recognised as Bernie the Boatman.

"Hmm, planning another fishing trip, is he?" asked Lottie, removing her shoes to avoid getting sand on the blanket.

"I hope so," said Sandra, "he really enjoys it and I think his liking of Bernie is a great asset to this holiday. He talks of him frequently and I almost feel that I know him too."

Hetty cast her eyes in the direction of the two men chatting beside a boat called the *Millicent Anne* which she assumed belonged to Bernie. "Let's go and introduce ourselves," she said.

Lottie looked puzzled. "But I thought you had him down as a likely suspect regarding Faith's death. In which case, why would you want to meet him?"

Hetty tutted. "For the very reason you've just stated." She stood up. "Come on, Lottie, put your shoes back on and let's go and suss out my number one suspect."

Lottie muttered under her breath as she picked up her shoes.

"So who's your number two suspect?" Sandra asked, tongue firmly in cheek.

Hetty bit her bottom lip. "Well, umm, to be honest I haven't found one yet but trust me, I'm working on it, Sandra. I just need the opportunity to meet more people."

Bernie they discovered was fifty-eight years old. He was also a charmer. He kissed both Lottie and Hetty on the backs of their hands and to their amazement flattered them shamelessly, referring to them as Bill's gorgeous little sisters thus taking them down a whole generation.

Hetty laughed and said, "Now, now, Bernie behave yourself." But her thoughts were focused on wondering if his sugary flirtatious banter, might indicate him to be one of the men with whom Faith had had an affair?

In the evening after they had eaten, all the family went to the Crown and Anchor. A local band were due to play and Sandra considered it might be good entertainment for Zac and the girls. It would also make a pleasant change for the rest of the family as long as the band weren't too loud.

The musicians were already there and busy setting up their equipment at the far end of the bar when the family seated themselves around a table. To Sandra's relief she saw that the band members were all young and handsome, and so she reckoned their good looks alone should meet with the approval of her daughters even if their music wasn't quite up to scratch.

As the band began to play, Hetty spotted Emma from the café tapping her feet to the music along with other young people and so in between songs she asked Emma to come and meet her family and especially her great nieces and nephew. Zac, glad to discover people of a similar age to himself, was thrilled when Emma asked him and his sisters to join her and her friends near to where the band were performing.

After an hour, the band stopped playing for a fifteen minute interval to enable them to refill their glasses and take a rest. Meanwhile, two of the pub's waitresses brought round complimentary cocktail pasties for the pub's patrons.

"Wow, that's very kind," said Hetty, taking a pasty and a paper napkin from a silver platter. "Thank you very much, dear."

Bill also took a pasty but Lottie and Sandra declined.

"Ashley is a fine looking chap, isn't he?" said Lottie, as the waitresses moved on to the next table, "and Alison must be besotted with him as she can hardly keep her eyes off him."

Sandra laughed. "Probably not been married very long then."

"Well actually according to Bernie," said Bill, "Ashley…oh never mind. Forget I said anything."

"Ashley what?" whispered Hetty, brushing pastry crumbs from her mouth.

Sandra nodded. "Yes, come on, Bill, you can't leave us guessing like this."

Bill glanced around to make sure no-one was in earshot. "Well, according to Bernie, Ashley had an affair with Faith not long ago but not many people know, or if they do they choose not to talk about it."

Hetty's jaw dropped. "Are you sure?"

Bill nodded. "That's what I was told."

"And you never thought to mention it before," said Hetty, clearly outraged.

"Well no. I mean, it's probably exaggerated anyway."

"No smoke without fire," muttered Hetty.

Sandra glanced across to the bar. "Does Alison know?" she asked, watching the young landlady hand a pint of cider to a customer.

Bill looked embarrassed and clearly wished he'd kept his mouth shut. "I suppose so, well yes, she must do but I didn't ask any questions because I'm not really one for gossip."

"Humph, so how come this Bernie knows?" said Hetty.

"He heard it on the grapevine. You see, apparently it cropped up during the police investigation regarding Faith's death. They questioned everyone with whom she'd had a relationship because they were obviously looking for anyone with a motive."

"And seemingly still are," said Lottie.

"So which of them ended the affair?" Hetty asked, keen to know every little detail.

"No idea," said Bill.

"So they must have questioned poor Alison thinking of her as a suspect," said Sandra, aghast, "how embarrassing for the poor woman. I hope she already knew or it would have been a terrible shock."

Lottie nodded. "I hope she had a good alibi too."

"She did," said Bill, "I do know that. Apparently she was here all morning. In fact she opened up and several people can vouch for that."

Hetty glanced towards the bar and frowned. "And how about Ashley? Does he have a good alibi too?"

Bill shrugged his shoulders. "No idea."

"Why on earth might he need one?" Lottie asked.

Hetty wiped her mouth and then her hands on the paper napkin. "Because if he ended the relationship, Faith might have threatened to tell Alison. That's why."

Chapter Ten

On Sunday morning Lottie woke up early, sat up in bed and looked from the window. The morning was bright and clear, the sea sparkled in the sunlight and birds in the garden of the bungalow next door, sang from the branches of a cherry tree. Lottie promptly made up her mind that she would go to church.

Across the room in her corner, Hetty stirred. Lottie told her sister of her decision and asked if she would like to go too. Hetty groaned; having had a little more wine the previous evening than she was used to, she declined the invitation and said perhaps she might go the following Sunday.

Two hours later when Lottie arrived back at the cottage after church, the family, having eaten breakfast, were sitting outside enjoying the sun. The grown-up on the lawn and the children around a picnic table on the patio.

Acknowledging the return of her mother-in-law, Sandra promptly jumped up from a garden chair and offered Lottie her seat. "Did you have any breakfast before you went, Mum?"

"Thank you," said Lottie, accepting the chair, "and yes, I had a slice of toast so I'm fine."

"Well, I'm sure you could drink a cup of tea."

"Oh, yes, that would be nice. Singing is thirsty work, although I didn't do a great deal I must admit but that was because I'd never heard one of the hymns before in my life and another one that I was familiar with they sang to a completely different tune."

"Probably just as well because you don't have a very good singing voice," Hetty teased.

Lottie scowled. "Having just been to church and feeling in a forgiving mood I shall ignore that comment, Hetty Tonkins."

Sandra paused in the conservatory doorway and waited for a break in the conversation before she asked if anyone else wanted tea: she then went off to the kitchen to put the kettle on.

"Were there many there?" Bill asked, folding up the Sunday paper and dropping it on the grass.

Lottie shook her head. "Not really. More than I thought there would be though and of course a few of them might have been holiday makers." She took off her lightweight jacket and hung it on the back of the chair. "It was really nice because the church door was left wide open during the service and so we were able to hear the sea and the cry of the gulls during the quiet bits. Just like we can here. I know it's silly, but I felt near to your father while I was there and I know he was with me in spirit. The church is lovely inside, quite big too and being able to hear the sea was very calming." Her eyes misted over. "Whenever we went on holiday, especially in later years when there was just the two of us, your dad would sit on the beach for ages, just watching the waves and listening to the sea tumbling and splashing. Deep in thought, he'd be. Bless him."

Bill reached out and gently patted his mother's hand. "I'm sorry, I should have gone with you this morning. I feel a cad now for not having been up."

Lottie smiled. "You're on holiday, Bill. You work hard and deserve a rest, and nine o'clock is rather early to be out by on a Sunday morning."

"I'll second that," said Hetty, peering over the top of her sunglasses, "it's far too early, especially when you've been out the night before."

Bill grinned. "Yes, but next week I'll try and make sure I'm up in time and go with you."

"Was there anyone there you knew?" Sandra asked, returning with a tray of tea cups which she placed on the picnic table.

Lottie nodded. "Yes, one or two. Louise was there sitting with a man who was no doubt her potter friend, Malcolm something or other who Chloe told us about. I had a chance to have a quick word with her after the service, Louise that is, and I told her how sorry we all were to hear of her son's tragic death. She said to thank you all. Poor soul, she was as white as a sheet."

"Very sad," said Bill, "I should imagine she's still in shock."

Lottie nodded her thanks to Sandra who handed her a cup of tea. "Yes, I daresay she is."

"Malcolm Biggins," said Hetty, waving her finger, "that's the name of Louise's potter chap."

Lottie nodded. "Yes, of course, and a fine looking man he is too. In fact he'd fit perfectly into the category of tall, dark and handsome, although I suppose he wouldn't really because his hair is a light sandy brown."

"In which case you must point him out to me if he crosses our path," said Hetty.

"Where does he do his potting?" Bill asked.

Lottie shook her head. "I don't know. We didn't ask, did we, Het?"

"No, but I shall try and find out as he may well need to go onto my list of suspects, even if he is good looking. In fact, his good looks might well earn him the position of number two on my suspect list."

Lottie looked uncomfortable. "I learned something else this morning but I'm not really sure whether or not I should tell. You see, Maisie from the charity shop was in church and she said…." Lottie suddenly stopped and shook her head. "No, no, I mustn't say more. It just doesn't seem right."

Hetty leaned forwards in the chair. "You can't tell half a tale, Lottie. You started and so you must finish as we're all intrigued now."

Lottie opened her mouth but then quickly closed it again.

"Come on, it'll not go beyond these four garden walls," persisted Hetty. "What did Maisie say?"

Lottie knew Hetty would sulk if she refused to divulge her news. "It's not very nice and Maisie told me in very hushed tones, I must add." Lottie lowered her head and wrung her hands, trying to find the right words. "The thing is…well…yesterday afternoon Maisie was in the café talking to Chloe who told her that the police now think Barry's death was suicide."

Hetty gasped. "No, surely not. Whatever gives them that idea?"

"Well, apparently it's because yesterday Louise went onto that Facebook thing you all like. Something she'd not done for several days, I might add. And on it she found a message from Barry that was sent on Tuesday night; the night he died and it said something

64

like: *Hi Mum, thanks for everything you've ever done for me. You've been brilliant but I can't go on. I'm sorry. Please forgive me. Luv Baz xx.* It was something like that. I don't expect for a minute I've got it anywhere near right but then only the last bit matters anyway."

Sandra's eyes filled with tears. "But that's dreadful. Poor, poor, Louise. Whatever could have made him do such a thing?"

"And what do you mean by only the last bit matters?" Hetty asked.

Lottie took a sip of tea. "I was just coming to that. You see, Louise doesn't think the message was sent by Barry because at the end he wrote *Luv Baz* which she says just doesn't ring true. She never called him Baz, you see, simply because she doesn't like that name in spite of the fact it's what nearly everyone else in the village used to call him. She was very fussy, Chloe can vouch for that, and because Louise didn't like the name Baz, Chloe always referred to Barry as Barry so that she didn't offend his mum."

Bill frowned. "Hmm, that certainly does seem a bit odd. I mean, if he knew his mother disliked it then it seems a little strange that he should have called himself Baz on the very last message she'd ever have from him."

Hetty was also intrigued. "I agree. Has Louise told the police of her concerns?"

Lottie nodded. "Yes, she rang them straight away, but they said the message was definitely sent from Barry's phone, which incidentally they only found yesterday morning as it had fallen into a crevice in the rocks and so they'd had great difficulty locating it."

"Didn't they try calling his number?" said Sandra. "Had they done that they would have known exactly where to locate it when it rang."

"Yes, they did try," said Lottie, "but apparently his battery had gone flat."

Sandra nodded. "Oh, I see."

"Anyway," Lottie continued, "the police are pretty confident that the message was sent by Barry. They checked the phone for fingerprints but only his were on it and so as far as they're concerned there's no reason to doubt its authenticity."

The conversation caught the imagination of Vicky who was sitting on the lawn painting her toe nails. "Perhaps he was forced to send the message by someone holding a gun to his head," she said, "and then afterwards the person holding the gun threw him off the cliff and his phone slipped into the crevice as he fell into the sea."

Kate gasped. "Oh yes. I bet he was having an affair with a married woman and when whoever she was dumped him he threatened to tell her husband and so she had no choice, she had to get rid of him."

"Or maybe the married woman's husband did find out about the affair and killed him to get his revenge," said Vicky, wriggling her toes and admiring her handiwork.

"Or perhaps Barry killed Faith and couldn't live with the guilt," said Kate, "There are numerous possibilities."

"My goodness me," said Lottie, shocked by her granddaughters' remarks, "what terrible, terrible things to say. Please don't go around expressing such opinions outside these garden walls. The locals would be dreadfully offended and quite rightly too."

"Hmm, yes," said Hetty, slowly, as she digested the twins' comments, "on the other hand, Lottie, there might well be something in what the girls say."

Vicky's jaw dropped in surprise. "Wow, do you really think so, Auntie?"

Hetty slowly and thoughtfully drummed her fingers on the arm of her chair. "I don't know, but something certainly doesn't ring true and I've had a feeling in my bones that something isn't right ever since I got here." She took in a deep breath. "If only we knew the local people better. If we did it might give us an insight into whether or not there could have been foul play. I think I might have to do a bit of serious investigating."

Lottie looked alarmed. "Be careful, Het. If people hear you say things like that you could become a target. It's one thing to jest that poor old Bernie the Boatman might be a guilty man and pretend you're making a list of suspects, within this family, but it's a different matter when you seriously threaten to poke your nose in where it's not wanted."

"Mum's right," Bill agreed. "If Barry was murdered then there are possibly two murderers in our midst and you don't want to get on the wrong side of either of them."

The family stayed at the cottage in the evening and Sandra with Bill's help cooked a roast dinner. As the time approached nine, Sandra said she would like to watch Andy Murray's match in the men's tennis singles final at the Olympic Games. She was confident he'd win a gold medal as he had done four years earlier in London 2012.

The match started around nine o'clock and when it got to half past ten, Hetty who didn't like tennis and couldn't stop yawning, said that she must go to bed. But she was the only one. Everyone else was determined to stay until the end. The match lasted for four hours and so it was half past one before they finally went to bed; but at least they were happy because Andy won.

Chapter Eleven

On Monday morning, Hetty woke up bright and early. The sun was shining in through the bedroom window and there appeared to be very little wind. Hetty looked at Lottie who was fast asleep in her corner and decided that she would leave her sister sleeping and take a stroll along the beach alone.

The cottage was quiet as Hetty crept downstairs. She thought about making a cup of tea but the draw of getting outside was greater than the need to quench her insignificant thirst.

She left the house by way of the conservatory, and found that already there was warmth in the early morning sun. With a spring in her step she walked through the garden, sniffing the flowers and watching the bees at work as she made her way along the path towards the steps which led down to the beach.

To Hetty's delight the beach was completely deserted. The shop was still closed and the empty boats stood in a row awaiting the day's activities to begin. With haste, she walked down to the water's edge and marvelled at the soothing rhythm of the waves gently falling onto the soft sand.

Suddenly she felt the urge to dance, and so singing and twirling she skipped along the shore until she was out of breath. When she stopped she felt giddy and sat down on a patch of shingle. She laughed, for life it seemed at that brief moment had reached a new high and everything around her looked rosy.

When her breath was restored and her legs had ceased wobbling, she stood and returned to the cottage, where she happily sang as she laid the table for breakfast hoping that by doing so she might wake up the rest of the family. Her ploy worked and one by one the family members entered the dining room and took their seats round the table, each one bleary eyed and listless after their late night.

"Does anyone want anything from the charity shop?" Hetty brightly asked, still very much in high spirits.

Bill's response was a cross between laughter and a yawn. "Don't tell me. You're looking for an excuse to visit the shop to further interrogate the two old dears who work in there."

Hetty looked most offended. "Actually, the two ladies of whom you speak are of a similar age to Lottie and myself, so less of the *old* please, William. But yes, you're quite right, they're the obvious people to question; they've lived in the village all their lives and there's not much goes on without their knowledge."

"Nor dare it by the sound of things," said Bill, amused that his aunt had derisively called him William.

Lottie smiled. "I daresay you're right, Bill. They're like old time village elders and thankfully are always willing to share the latest gossip."

"Exactly," said Hetty, stirring sugar into her tea, "and so for that reason they'll think we're just being nosy rather than trying to glean incriminating information from them in order to catch a killer."

"Or two," Lottie added.

Bill tutted and looked heavenwards.

"Perhaps you could get a glass from the charity shop to replace the one that Mum broke," said Kate, pouring cereal into a bowl. "Save her buying a new one."

"A glass," said Lottie, "what sort of glass?"

Sandra looked embarrassed. "A beer glass. I broke it when I was washing up yesterday morning. It would have been while you were at church. It was just an ordinary straight sided pint glass but I really feel I ought to replace it."

"Excellent," said Hetty, gleefully rubbing her hands, "we'll do our best."

Sandra nodded. "Well, I hope you're lucky. I shan't be here when you get back because I'm taking the girls to Newquay so they can try their hand at surfing. In fact I daresay we won't be back much before six."

"In which case we'll have dinner at the pub again tonight," said Bill. "Save us cooking and all that. I'm going on a fishing trip with Bernie later so I shall be feeling pretty peckish."

"And to make sure we have an appetite, Lottie and I shall probably go for a nice long walk this afternoon."

"Anywhere in particular?" Sandra asked.

Hetty shrugged her shoulders. "We'll decide later."

"Which mean," said Bill, "it all depends what you learn from your friends in the charity shop."

When they arrived at the shop the two sisters were dismayed to find no sign of Maisie or Daisy. Behind the counter stood a tall man with thinning hair who was laughing and joking with a customer as he dropped her purchase into an old carrier bag. The sisters stood speechless beside a display of beachwear, their disappointment and annoyance made worse by the strange man's irritating laugh.

Feeling that they ought to act as normally as possible, Hetty browsed through a rack of skirts and Lottie looked at the shelves of kitchenware. To her surprise she saw several pint glasses any of which could replace the one broken at the cottage. She pointed them out to Hetty but both agreed they would leave it as an excuse to call again another day when hopefully Maisie and Daisy would be back on duty, but so they didn't leave empty handed and to give them a reason to speak to the strange man, Lottie bought another paperback book and took it to the counter.

"I take it that Maisie and Daisy are not working today," said Lottie, as she fished out a fifty pence piece from her purse.

"Nope," said the strange man, who spoke with a soft Irish accent. "They both have Monday off one week and then Wednesday the next. I work when they're off on a Monday and Cilla works when they're off on a Wednesday." He gave the sisters a puzzled look. "Are they friends of yours? I don't think I've seen you two lovely ladies before."

"No, no, we just know them from when we've visited the shop," said Hetty. "We're on holiday, you see, and staying at Sea View Cottage."

"Ah, begorra, that'll be lecherous Lance's place," said the stranger.

"Lecherous Lance?" repeated Lottie, taken back by his comment, "I mean, is he…you know…what you just called him?"

"Not half," said the stranger. "You never see him with the same woman twice."

"Oh, how interesting and have he and Rosie Rutherford ever been romantically linked?" Hetty asked, even though she already knew that Chloe reckoned their relationship was purely platonic.

"No, Rosie's not Lance's type, although he did have a dalliance with her friend and next door neighbour, Faith...poor kid. He goes for glamour, you see, and so you two ladies had better watch out if he decides to pay a visit while you're here."

In the afternoon Lottie and Hetty decided to utilise the beautiful weather and take a walk along the coastal path. Because Zac had mentioned that Rosie's workshop in the old lifeboat house lay just over the cliffs where it was tucked inside a small cove, they walked in an easterly direction so they might see for themselves. To their horror, en route they encountered part of the cliff path had been cordoned off with blue and white police tape.

"Oh no, how silly. It never occurred to me that we'd pass this spot," said Lottie, clearly upset. "I've gone all shivery and light headed." She sat down on the grass and Hetty sat beside her.

"I know how you feel and it's difficult to imagine a beautiful spot like this being the place where poor Barry lost his life," said Hetty, "whether it be his own doing or that of someone else." She shuddered. "I don't know if it's my imagination but the air seems to be tinged with sadness here, almost ghostlike. You know, it's like Barry's here...watching."

"And looking for answers," said Lottie, sadly, "If he is here he'll be looking for answers, Het, and wanting to know why he died."

Hetty turned to face her sister. "You believe the lad was killed then?"

Lottie nodded. "Yes, I do, and I think it's because of the message he supposedly sent to his mother. I can't help but feel there's something in what Louise says about the name."

"Any reason why you think that?"

Lottie sat quietly, absentmindedly watching a loose strip of police tape as it flapped in the breeze.

"Yes," she said, realising she had been asked a question, "there is. You see, many years ago when Bill and Barbara were at school,

71

Barbara's friends called her Barbie and I really didn't like it. For that reason Barbara always made a point of never referring to herself as Barbie when in my presence and likewise asking her friends to do the same. So in a way I can put myself in Louise's shoes, so to speak."

"I didn't know that," said Hetty, "you know, about the Barbie thing. I mean, I've never thought of her as anything other than Barbara."

"Well, I suppose you never really saw much of her school friends and so wouldn't have heard it. To be honest, it only went on for a few years and after she left school she reverted to being Barbara, thank goodness, and has called herself that ever since."

After the fishing trip, Bill knowing his wife and daughters were unlikely to be back from Newquay for a while, popped into the Crown and Anchor for a quick pint with Bernie the Boatman. Being late afternoon, the pub was quiet and so they sat on stools at the bar. Ashley Rowe, the landlord, was on duty and topping up a stand of leaflets featuring local artists Rosie Rutherford and Malcolm Biggins the Potter as well as others whose names were unfamiliar to Bill.

"I hear Rosie's talking of giving up painting," said Bernie, nodding towards the leaflets. "Apparently her eyesight's starting to fade and I noticed she was wearing glasses the other day."

Ashley grunted. "She has my sympathy then. Mine's gone downhill fast since we transferred all the pub's paperwork onto the wretched computer. Having said that, I'm not getting any younger and both my parents were wearing specs at my age so I can't really complain."

"Same here," agreed Bill, rubbing his finger through the condensation on the side of his pint glass, "I blame the invention of the mobile phone for my worsening eyesight. Everything on it is so damn small."

Ashley nodded. "Yes, and that as well."

"Might be worth snapping up a few of Rosie's paintings then if she's not likely to do any more," said Bernie, thoughtfully tapping his fingers on the surface of the bar. "Could be a good investment."

"Hmm, that thought had just crossed my mind," said Ashley. "Could be a good little nest-egg. I mean, it's not really worth saving money nowadays, is it? Not with the interest rate being so low."

Bernie agreed "Absolutely. We've put most of our spare money into Premium Bonds but we seldom win more than the occasional twenty five pounds. Still, you never know, we might be lucky one day."

"There's one of Rosie's pictures in our cottage," said Bill, wishing he had spare money to invest in Premium Bonds or to buy a painting, "I must admit it's very good."

"Does it have the two penguins on it?" Bernie asked.

"Yes. Sandra and the girls think they're really cute."

"That'll be one of her more recent ones then," said Bernie, "I mean, what she does now is so much better than that crap she did a few years back."

Bill frowned. "Which was?"

"Modern stuff," said Bernie, a look of disdain on his face. "You know, the sort of thing that looks like it were done by a kid while throwing a tantrum. That's what she used to do when she first moved here and to be fair she had a good name too. But then she changed her style. She said it was the influence of the beautiful scenery. Too beautiful not to want to capture it, so I can't fault her there."

"Well she's able to do that alright," said Bill, after taking several sips of beer, "the one in our cottage is of Saint Michael's Mount and it's absolutely brilliant. The colours are quite superb."

"Is it the original or a print?" Ashley asked.

"Hmm, I've no idea," said Bill, "I mean until you asked I'd assumed it was original but on reflection I suppose it's most likely a print. I mean, it would be a bit risky to put the original in a cottage that stands empty for part of the year."

"It stands empty for most of the year," said Ashley, "although Lance did let it out for a while last winter. From sometime in January until Easter I think it was."

Bernie chortled. "Oh yeah, I'd forgotten the bank robbers. How could I do that?"

Bill nearly choked on his beer. "Bank robbers. Surely not."

Ashley shook his head. "No, they weren't really but some smart aleck named them that because neither of them seemed to be working yet both had plenty of money to throw around. They came in here a lot and always bought drinks for you locals. If I remember correctly they claimed to be down here looking at property for a business opportunity but they never said what it was."

Bernie chuckled. "No, but it sounds good, doesn't it?"

"Yes, and it's most likely a euphemism for taking a very long holiday." said Ashley. "What were their names? I can't remember even though I'm usually pretty good at remembering names."

"Doug and Don," Bernie promptly answered. "Doug had a shaven head and was the more talkative of the two. Don had long dark hair and a beard; he seemed quite reticent. And if you remember, Doug was the one who kept trying to chat up Faith but she was having none of it and kept him at arm's length."

Ashley frowned and with unnecessary vigour wiped down the bar in order to hide his obvious embarrassment. Bill made a mental note of his action and also details regarding Doug and Don as he thought the information might be appreciated by his mother and his aunt.

Chapter Twelve

Tuesday morning dawned dull but by mid-morning the sun was shining brightly and the day felt warm. With every intention of spending some time on the beach, Sandra went out to the car to fetch her sunglasses from the glove compartment. As she closed the car door she glanced across the road and saw Rosie Rutherford sitting on a bench outside the church. Rosie waved and called out, "Still enjoying your holiday, I hope."

Sandra placed the sunglasses on top of her head and crossed the road. "Yes, thank you. In fact, we're all extremely happy. The cottage is absolutely gorgeous. Comfortable too, and the garden is beautiful and puts mine back home to shame."

"That's nice to hear," said Rosie, "I know Lance has spent a lot of money on it over the years. It was in a bad way when he bought it, you see. The roof leaked and so the place was very damp. The owner before Lance was an elderly gentleman, so I believe, who had no family. I've heard it said that he was a bit odd but it was before I lived here so the poor chap was probably just a loner. Anyway, after his demise the house stood empty for a year or two and so got even more damp. Eventually solicitors tracked down a nephew who on hearing of his inheritance promptly sold it."

"Poor house," said Sandra, sitting down beside Rosie, "but I'm sure it's much loved now and especially by people such as ourselves who are fortunate enough to have use of it for a holiday."

"Yes, I'm sure you're right. It's certainly a choice spot."

"So may I ask how long you've lived in Pentrillick?"

Rosie thought for a few moments. "Must be about five years now. Good heavens, it doesn't seem as long as that. How time flies."

Sandra suddenly remembered Barry. "We were very sorry to hear that the poor lad who died last week took his life. His poor mother. I can't even begin to imagine what she must be going through."

Rosie nodded. "I know; it's dreadful, isn't it? I didn't really know Barry other than by sight, but I've spoken to his mother many times as I often pop in the café. Poor Louise, such a cruel thing to have inflicted on one. And so sad for the village too. For him to have died so soon after the dreadful murder of poor Faith is very cruel and quite difficult to comprehend."

"I've heard Faith was a friend of yours."

"Yes, she was a very good friend and my next door neighbour too." Rosie half-smiled. "To get her out of the house I often took her with me to my studio. She loved that. She'd sit outside on the slipway in the sun and watch the world go by. Dear Faith...I do miss her."

As Sandra returned to the cottage, she met Hetty and Lottie who were on their way to the charity shop. They exchanged a few words and then the sisters continued along the now familiar route.

To their delight, Maisie and Daisy were both on duty and unpacking bags of clothing which had been left outside on the doorstep. After greeting each other, Lottie picked up a couple of pint glasses and took them to the counter.

"You've saved my daughter-in-law's bacon," said Lottie. "She broke a glass similar to these in the cottage the other day and now we're able to replace it."

Hetty looked over her sister's shoulder. "But why are you buying two?"

"In case she or someone else breaks another, of course."

"Hmm, good thinking," said Maisie, "but it has to be said that if another glass gets broken it's bound to be entirely different from this."

Daisy nodded. "Yes, Murphy's law."

"Murphy, yes, that reminds me," said Hetty, "we popped in here yesterday and were told by the Irish chap that you both had the day off."

"Irish chap," said Daisy, with a laugh, "that'll be Tommy Thomas. He covers for us every other Monday. He's not Irish though, he's a Cornishman but for a laugh he speaks in an Irish accent from time to time, especially when dealing with strangers."

"Oh, I see, well he had us fooled," said Hetty, thinking Tommy sounded a little odd. "So is he a local chap?"

"Yes and no. He's local inasmuch as he's from West Cornwall, Lamorna in fact and I reckon he's been in Pentrillick for about twelve months now. What say you, Maisie?"

"Hmm, possibly a bit more than twelve, I'd say more like eighteen."

Hetty wanted to ask if he was married but knew if she did it might sound as though she was seeking a mate. To her delight Daisy volunteered the information sought without her needing to say a word.

"He's a crusty old bachelor and still lives with his aged mother," said Daisy, "but his heart's in the right place. His dad died several years ago so we've been told and so his mother is glad of his company."

"More than several," corrected Maisie, "I believe Tommy was only in his twenties when he lost his dad and he's in his sixties now."

Daisy frowned. "Was he? Oh well, that's neither here nor there."

Hetty quickly digested the information received and wondered if she ought to add Tommy to her fanciful suspect list.

"Have you been to Pentrillick House yet?" Maisie suddenly asked, as she peeled price stickers off the glasses.

"Yes, and we were very impressed," said Lottie. "Beautiful location and so we shall no doubt go again."

"And the other day we took a walk up Long Lane to see where Rosie lives," said Hetty, "and we very much admired the views. They're quite breath-taking."

"Yes, it's very nice up there," said Daisy, "although it does catch the wind but then you can't have everything."

"There was a blue VW Beetle parked in front of Faith's garage," said Lottie. "Would we be right in assuming it had belonged to the poor lady?"

"That's right, it did," said Maisie, carefully wrapping both glasses in sheets of tissue. "She loved that little car and called it George but I don't know why."

"Oh, that's rather sweet," said Lottie, thinking of the Beatles and her childhood heartthrob, George Harrison.

Hetty gave a little cough and then casually asked, "Are there…umm… any more developments regarding her death?"

Daisy shrugged her shoulders. "None whatsoever as far as I know and the same goes for young Barry. I don't know what goes on. We're all as mystified as each other."

Maisie passed the glasses to Lottie. "But as I said in church on Sunday, the police reckon Barry's death was suicide."

Both sisters nodded and Lottie paid for the glasses.

"Yes, but you also said that Louise doesn't think the message was sent by Barry because he referred to himself as Baz," said Lottie. "It all seems very strange to me."

"And to us as well," said Daisy, folding her arms, "and I must admit it gives me the creeps thinking about that horrid call poor Barry had, which according to the coppers would have been just before he died." She shuddered. "It's really spine-chilling."

"Call," said Hetty, "what call?"

"To his mobile phone," said Daisy. "Haven't you heard about that? The police discovered it when they were checking out the Facebook message to Louise."

Hetty and Lottie both shook their heads.

"Well, as I say, the police reckon he got the call just before he died. He couldn't have answered it though because it was listed as a missed call." Daisy paused momentarily and took a deep breath. "The call was from Faith's missing mobile phone."

Hetty and Lottie left the shop and headed back towards the cottage in a daze, both shocked after hearing of the missed call. For both agreed it was beyond comprehension to imagine how Barry must have felt on seeing who the missed call was from.

"Someone must have done it to scare the lad," said Lottie, "but why?"

"And what an inopportune moment," said Hetty. "I can't help but wonder if it might in some way have caused him to fall to his death."

Lottie shook her head. "No, because the message he allegedly sent to Louise was sent after the missed call and so it must have taken him a minute or two to send it. That's if it was him which I very much doubt."

"I wish in some way all this helped to fit the jigsaw together but it doesn't help at all, does it?" said Hetty.

"No, although it does help inasmuch as we now know that whoever killed Faith and took her phone must also have known Barry otherwise why would he or she have rung his number?"

Hetty shook her head. "It doesn't prove that at all, Lottie. After all, Faith no doubt has lots of numbers stored on her phone and so the murderer might simply have selected one randomly and rung it just to wind up the police knowing whoever received it was bound to report it."

"So we're none the wiser," said Lottie. "What a nightmare."

As they neared the cottage, a black VW Beetle drove past. Hetty stopped walking and watched as the car continued down the street and then disappeared round a bend. To Lottie's surprise she saw that Hetty was frowning.

"What's the matter, Het? You look even more puzzled now."

"Yes, and that's because a thought just struck me - seeing that car, the Beetle, I mean. Naturally it reminded me of Faith and I wonder, Lottie, do you think it's possible that the person who murdered Faith might have gone to her cottage with the sole intention of killing her and *not* to steal the money."

Lottie shook her head. "No, that can't be the case because if you remember Faith's car wasn't there, it'd gone in for its MOT which means the murderer would have assumed that she wasn't in. And if he thought she wasn't in then he wouldn't have bothered going in to kill her, would he?"

Hetty's shoulders slumped. "No, of course not. I keep forgetting that's why everyone thinks it was attempted robbery which went wrong because the robber-cum-murderer thought her to be out when actually she was at home."

Lottie nodded. "Precisely."

"On the other hand," persisted Hetty, as she began to walk again but very slowly, "maybe that's what we're supposed to think and the person in question knew that her car was having its MOT done."

It was Lottie's turn to stop. "Hmm, feasible, I suppose. Anyone who worked at the garage, for instance. They would know."

"It's more than possible, Lottie, and for that reason I think it might be worth our while checking it out. We know there's a garage just outside the village because we passed it the other day on the bus. We must go there and do a bit of snooping."

"What now?"

"Yes, once you've dropped those glasses back at the cottage. After all we've nothing else planned for today."

Lottie smiled. "Okay, so we'll do as you suggest and walk to the garage, but what can be our purpose? I mean, we can't go and get petrol with our only mode of transport being the cottage bikes."

Hetty groaned. "Damn, I hadn't thought of that. I wonder if the garage has a shop."

"I can't say that I noticed one but it might be worth walking out there on the off-chance. We can always lurk around nearby on the pretence of picking blackberries or looking for bird's nests. Something like that."

"Bird's nests in August. Wake up, Lottie."

"Oh, yes…silly me. You know what I mean though."

When the sisters called in at the cottage to leave the two glasses, they found to their relief that everyone was out and so they had no need to say where they were going. A note on the table informed them that Sandra and the girls were on the beach; Bill and Zac had gone shopping in Penzance.

The sisters walked back through the village and after passing the Crown and Anchor they followed the road around a bend where the village primary school, quiet due to the summer holiday, stood well back from the road. After the school they passed a car park and walking out from it was a man unfamiliar to Hetty. Lottie, however, recognised him and with a nod of her head and a nudge with her elbow told Hetty in a whisper that he was Malcolm Biggins the potter and partner of Barry's mother, Louise who worked at the café. Hetty was delighted, for seeing him meant she had another face to add to her short list of suspects.

After the car park they were out into the open countryside and from the lane, glimpses of the sea were visible in places through farm gateways and over dry stone walls. The narrow lane twisted and turned past a farm and fields where sheep grazed on the lush green grass: past a lone cottage where free range eggs were boxed up for sale on the doorstep and past a sign indicating a bridle path which ran down to the sea.

The garage lay just under a mile outside the village at the end of the lane and situated on the corner of a junction with the main road.

To the delight of the sisters, a huge board advertised MOTs and there was a shop. Eagerly passing two cars filling up with petrol on the forecourt, Hetty and Lottie went inside the shop hopeful that there might be things over which they could browse and keep a watchful eye out for any suspicious looking characters.

The shop was small and most of its merchandise was beach orientated, much like the shop on the beach at Pentrillick, but it did sell a few groceries and had a good range of sweets. Hetty and Lottie picked up a wire basket and while lingering over the confectionary, conveniently situated near to the window, they watched the comings and goings at the garage workshop where they assumed MOTs might be done. To their dismay there was very little to see. A young lad went into the workshop and a cat came out. A passing car tooted to one of the people on the forecourt and a tractor drove by on the main road with a steady flow of traffic stuck behind it. Shortly after, the drivers of the two cars on the forecourt came into the shop, paid for their fuel and then drove off. As they disappeared from view, a small truck drove in. Lottie sighed and dropped a bag of mint humbugs into their shopping basket, feeling that they were on a wild goose chase. And then suddenly a man and a woman walked out from the workshop chatting. Lottie frowned. "Look, Het, does that chap in the boiler suit look familiar to you?"

Hetty smiled. "Hmm, well to be honest, he does look like a young Prince Charles." She squinted. "In fact were we able to wind the clock back a few years, I'd say it was Prince Charles."

"Yes, but we are not in a few years back, Het, we're in 2016. I wonder who he is."

"A distant cousin perhaps," said Hetty, with hope.

"I doubt it. Come on, let's pay for these sweets and get out there to hear what's being said."

The woman had her back towards Hetty and Lottie as they stepped outside, and after she and Prince Charles had finished speaking, he opened the door of her silver Audi and the woman slipped into the driver's seat. As she drove away, Hetty caught sight of her face.

"That was Alison, the pub's landlady," she said, "well I never."

Lottie laughed. "Well, I suppose she needs work done to her car the same as anyone else."

But Hetty didn't answer because Prince Charles was looking their way.

"Good afternoon," Hetty called in her best telephone voice, "beautiful day."

"Tis my 'ansome," said Prince Charles, in a gruff Cornish accent.

Hetty was rather taken back. Lottie giggled but her laughter quickly faded as a familiar Volvo estate drove onto the forecourt.

"Grandma and Auntie Hetty," said Zac, leaning from the front passenger window of the Volvo as Bill stepped from the car and reached for the petrol hose. "Look Dad."

When Bill turned around he was clearly surprised. "What on earth are you two doing right out here?"

"Us? Oh, we were…umm…just walking," said Lottie, "and then…umm…we saw the shop and so popped in for some sweets. Anyone for a humbug?"

Chapter Thirteen

It was agreed that the family would stay at the cottage on Tuesday evening and each have a pasty bought from a bakery earlier in the day by Bill and Zac while out shopping. They would, however, definitely go to the Crown and Anchor the following day because Bernie the Boatman had told Bill that Wednesday was quiz night and there was always a good turnout.

While the pasties were warming in the oven, Sandra fetched in washing from the line. Bill checked his emails: the girls watched the television. Zac, keen to look at pictures he'd recently taken of his new friends on a screen bigger than his mobile, plugged his phone into his mother's laptop.

As Sandra was folding up the washing she casually glanced over Zac's shoulder. The first pictures she saw were the ones he had taken overlooking Rosie's studio shortly after they'd first arrived.

"So is that the old lifeboat house?" she asked. "It looks very nice and what a lovely spot."

"Yep," said Zac, "and if you look carefully you can see Rosie talking to someone."

Sandra squinted. "Oh, yes, I see her. Who is she talking to I wonder? I can't see properly without my reading glasses."

Zac enlarged the picture. "Oh, that's weird," he said, "it looks like that poor bloke, Barry, who died the other day."

"How come you know what he looks like?" Vicky asked, "You never met him."

"No, I didn't, but Emma showed me a picture hanging in the pub of him with the pool team."

Sandra leaned forwards. "I think you're right, Zac. I never met him either but I did see when we went to Pentrillick House." She stood up straight. "It strikes me as a little odd though, because Rosie told me she didn't know him other than by sight."

Hetty, sitting on the sofa reading alongside her sister, promptly dropped her Kindle when she heard the comments and sprang to her feet. "What! Let me see, please, Zac."

"Oh yes, that's definitely young Barry," said Hetty, "I'd recognise that mop of hair anywhere. And you say Rosie claims she hardly knew him, Sandra?"

Sandra nodded.

Hetty's eyes twinkled. "Hmm, very interesting."

"Wow, it looks like I was right then," said Vicky, with a giggle, "he must have been having an affair after all and with old Rosie of all people. Fancy that."

"Surely not," said Sandra, returning her attention to the washing, "she must be twice Barry's age."

Vicky shrugged her shoulders. "Some older women, especially ones with plenty of money, like to have a toy-boy. Better than being stuck with fat middle-aged men, I suppose."

Zac tutted. "But Rosie isn't married, you numpty, so your theory that Barry was threatening to tell her husband just doesn't hold water."

Vicky pulled an unladylike face. "Hmm...well...maybe she's got a bloke who is possessive and we just don't know about him."

"Barry was a nice looking lad," said Lottie, thoughtfully, "I can't think of any reason why he'd have a dalliance with an older lady like Rosie when there are so many pretty young girls around."

"Money," suggested Hetty, as she sat back down on the settee. "I think that's a pretty good reason."

"No," said Lottie, emphatically, "I'm sure Barry wouldn't have been enticed by her money."

"I expect you'll find there's a perfectly innocent explanation, like he's delivering something from the garden centre," said Bill, putting on his glasses to take a look at the picture. "Yes, look," he added, pointing to the screen, "Rosie is holding a hanging basket. And if you look further back up the track there's a van parked with the Pentrillick Garden Centre written on the side." He laughed. "Really, you lot aren't very observant. Having said that, I must award you all ten out of ten for imagination, albeit overactive."

Lottie chuckled. "Come to think of it, when I was chatting to Maisie in church last Sunday, I remember her saying that recent wind had played havoc with her hanging baskets and that a couple of Rosie's had blown down too. I assumed she meant at her house but it looks like they were at the studio and young Barry was replacing them."

Hetty's shoulders slumped. "What a shame. I really thought we were onto something then."

"Do you think there might be a link between Barry's death and poor Faith's murder?" Sandra suddenly asked. "I mean, two suspicious deaths in a village in such a short space of time must be very unusual."

"I've wondered that too," said Hetty, "because if Louise's hunch is right and Barry didn't send the suicide message then there is every reason to suspect that he was murdered as well. I mean, if he fell then there would be no message, would there? It just doesn't make sense."

"But who and why would anyone do such a thing?" Sandra asked. "We know of a motive for Faith's murder but I can't for the life of me think of a reason for anyone to harm Barry. Not that we knew him of course."

Hetty, not wanting to let on that she and Lottie thought Faith's death was probably premeditated, thoughtfully stroked her chin. "I agree, although there is always the possibility that Barry thought he knew who murdered Faith and word got back to the guilty party."

Lottie frowned. "Meaning, Faith and Barry were both victims of the same person."

Hetty nodded. "Yes."

"I'd be interested to know what the police think," said Sandra. "We know they've said that the message must have be sent by Barry but is that what they actually believe?"

"Good point," said Lottie.

Bill listened to the conversation with an amused smile on his face. "I've just remembered something you ladies might find interesting. I meant to tell you yesterday but completely forgot."

"We're all ears," said Hetty, sitting forward on the settee.

Bill laughed. "I guessed you would be. Anyway, yesterday Bernie and I popped into the pub after we'd been fishing and during the conversation we had with Ashley the landlord I learned that last winter two chaps rented this cottage and they were here from some time in January until Easter."

Hetty's face lit up. "Really. What were they like? Why were they here?"

"From what I gathered no-one really got to know much about them except that they claimed they were here looking at property for a business venture or something like that. But whatever their reason, they spent a lot of time in the pub and it seems had money to burn. But the thing you'll be most interested in is the fact that one of them was rather taken with Faith Trethewy."

Hetty gasped but didn't speak.

"Faith," repeated Sandra.

Bill nodded. "Yes, and when Bernie mentioned it, Ashley went very quiet and aggressively rubbed down the bar clearly to hide his embarrassment."

"So what happened?" Lottie asked. "Did he and Faith ever get together?"

Bill shook his head. "Well, no, apparently not."

"Humph, that's a bit of an anti-climax then," said Hetty, punching the lumpy cushion by her side, "unless there's more tell."

Bill shrugged his shoulders. "I'm afraid there's not. It seems that Faith didn't want to know so that was the end of that."

Lottie sighed. "I wonder why not? From what we've heard she wasn't at all fussy."

As Vicky was about to ask Lottie to clarify her comment, Bill raised his hand as though at school. "Hang on, I just remembered something else. The two chaps were called Doug and Don and it was Doug who was interested in Faith. I remember that because there's a Doug at work."

"Doug and Don. Hmm, it might be worth looking into them," said Hetty.

Lottie frowned. "And just how do you intend to do that, Het? You don't know where they live or anything about them. What's more, the police will no doubt have checked them out already, even though they weren't even here in July when Faith was murdered."

Hetty frowned. "Yes, I suppose that does rule them out. Are you sure they went home at Easter, Bill? Wherever home might be."

Bill nodded. "That's what I was told and it sounds feasible as I daresay Lance had people coming to stay in here over the Easter break - it being the beginning of the holiday season and all that."

Hetty looked downcast. "Oh well, it's still food for thought."

"Oh, hang on, I've just remembered something else," Bill said with an impish chuckle, "apparently because the two blokes seemed loaded and spent money like water, one of the locals named them the Bank Robbers and the name seems to have stuck."

Hetty rubbed her hands. "Bank robbers," she chuckled, "the plot thickens."

Chapter Fourteen

Wednesday morning dawned dull beneath a blanket of grey sky and the forecast was for showers.

Bill, who had already booked a day's fishing with Bernie, said the weather wouldn't bother him and the conditions might even prove beneficial from a catch point of view.

Zac likewise said the weather didn't matter. He was going out to meet his new friends to play volleyball on the beach, having been inspired by the Olympics, and if the heavens opened they would spend a few hours in the pub playing pool.

The rest of the family were unsure how to spend the day until Sandra suggested going to a car boot sale that she had seen advertised at a place called Rosudgeon which was held every Wednesday.

Vicky and Kate weren't over-thrilled with the option but agreed it was better than staying indoors. Hetty and Lottie on the other hand thought the prospect of a morning trawling through all sorts of odds and ends very appealing.

They arrived at the car boot sale just after ten and parked in a football field which was rapidly filling up. On another field, sellers were unpacking goods from their cars and the smell of chips, burgers and coffee hung in the damp morning air.

Towards the top of the field, larger vans, already unpacked, were selling their wares and so the family made their way across the field to take a closer look. From one of the vans two young men were selling objects obtained from house clearances and after perusing the items, Lottie bought a large aspidistra plant in a very ornate replica Victorian planter. Hetty was not impressed.

"Why on earth have you bought that hideous thing, Lottie? Aspidistras are so old-fashioned and boring, they look the same year in year out and gather dust."

Lottie's mouth turned upside-down. "I bought it because it reminds me of Grandma. She had one if you remember. It stood in the middle of the square table in the best room on a thick brown tablecloth with a long fringe? It was huge."

"So is that thing, but I'm not sure whether Grandma's plant was huge or we were just small. Really, Lottie, you are such an old fuddy-duddy."

The twins were much amused to see their grandmother being ticked off by their great aunt. To stop them giggling Sandra handed them each a five pound note and sent them off to browse saying they all would meet up by the pavilion at eleven thirty.

As Hetty, Lottie and Sandra stopped to admire a colourful collection of rose bushes, they saw Rosie approaching carrying four attractive cushions. Her eyes opened wide like saucers when she saw the aspidistra. "Good heavens above, where did you get that? You don't see many of them around these days."

"Thank goodness," muttered Hetty.

"I bought it from some lads who do house clearances," said Lottie, fondly patting the replica Victorian planter, "the poor plant needs a bit of TLC. It might have died if no-one had bought it."

Hetty laughed. "Not likely. They don't call aspidistras cast iron plants for no reason."

"They do sometimes flower," said Lottie, in defence of her purchase. "I'm sure I read that somewhere."

Rosie wrinkled her nose. "Yes, mature plants have been known to flower but the flowers are quite insignificant and form at the base of the plant at soil level. I believe there's only ever one at a time and it lasts just a week or two."

Lottie looked hopeful. "Well, this is a mature plant so I can always dream that it might one day flower."

Rosie chuckled mischievously. "Well, if it does keep an eye on it as they're pollinated by slugs and snails."

"Ugh!" said Hetty, backing away from the plant and flapping her hands. "I didn't know that."

Lottie's face dropped. "Neither did I."

"So, are you intending to take it home with you or will you leave it in the cottage for others to enjoy?" Rosie asked, her face lit by a large smile as she tried not to giggle.

"Well, I was going to take it home," said Lottie, her nose twitching as though troubled by an unpleasant smell. "On the other hand, I might leave it behind."

"Good idea," said Hetty, "we don't want to be lumbered with that great thing on the train anyway. I should keep the planter though as it's quite attractive."

The rain held off all morning and at half eleven as planned they all met up by the pavilion.

Most of the twins' money had been spent on sweets, drinks and a few items of jewellery. Sandra held up a pair of sandals she'd bought for fifty pence. Lottie had nothing to show other than the aspidistra which was beginning to weigh heavy and Hetty had a bag of DVDs which she looked forward to watching during the long winter months.

The rain began mid-afternoon just after Bill arrived back from his fishing trip and by seven o'clock all were getting tired of being indoors. To relieve the boredom it was decided they would go to the Crown and Anchor early and have something to eat which would also guarantee they had seats for when the quiz began at nine o'clock.

The pub was already busy when they arrived with other families eating in the dining room and two bars but they managed to find a table near to a piano with sufficient capacity to seat them all.

By half past eight many of the other diners had left and the place was beginning to fill up with people arriving for the quiz.

Hetty and Lottie watched as the new arrivals filed in and were delighted when they saw anyone that they recognised.

They waved as Maisie and Daisy entered the bar with two men who they assumed were their husbands.

Soon after followed young Emma from the café and an older girl with similar features who they decided must be her sister.

Bernie arrived with a man who Hetty and Lottie instantly recognised as the young Prince Charles lookalike who they had seen at the garage. Bill waved to the latest arrivals.

"Who is that with Bernie?" Lottie asked, "Do you know him?"

"That's Vince," said Bill, "he owns the garage just outside the village. You know, where I picked you up yesterday."

"Yes, I know where you mean." She gave a little laugh. "I'm intrigued because Hetty and I saw him yesterday and we think he looks like a young Prince Charles."

"Yes, I agree there is a similarity and funnily enough his name is Vince Royale."

It was Hetty's turn to chuckle. "Prince Vince and he's a royal to boot. Well I never."

Before Hetty or Lottie had a chance to ask Bill for any other information about Vince, Tommy Thomas who worked in the charity shop every other Monday arrived with an elderly lady who they assumed to be his mother. And they were immediately followed by Rosie Rutherford and three other people of whose identity they had no idea.

Hetty took great interest in the people around her, eagerly looking for anyone whom she thought might have been involved in the death of either Faith or Barry or perhaps even both. Tommy Thomas sat with his mother, each drinking beer from half pint glasses. Were finances tight for the couple? She wondered. Tight enough for Tommy to attempt to rob Faith? Instantly she rebuked herself. People who stole seldom did so to put food on the table or to pay household bills. The motivation for robbery was usually pure greed, although it seemed that in the current era it was also a means to buying drugs or of obtaining cash to pay off pressing debt to unscrupulous people with unsympathetic ears.

She smiled when she saw Tommy's mother laughing and wondered if Tommy ever spoke to her in an Irish accent.

It was Chloe from the café who handed out the quiz sheets, thus enabling Hetty to enquire as to the identity of Rosie's friends. She was surprised to learn that one of the women was Samantha Liddicott-Treen. The other two were fellow artists who also had studios in West Cornwall.

Hetty tutted loudly as the information sank in. How could she not have recognised Samantha Liddicott-Treen? She had seen pictures of the lady on Pentrillick House website several times although admittedly her eyes had usually lingered longer over the features of her dashingly handsome husband, Tristan. But it had to be said that Samantha had fine features too. Beautiful dark wavy hair, a fine bone structure and a figure most women would die for. Even dressed in casual clothes, she was a picture of elegance.

To the family's relief the answers to the quiz questions were not beyond their capabilities, but the adults had to confess that without the children's input, questions on present day music and celebrities would have been impossible to answer. Likewise, Hetty and Lottie were a mine of information on the subject of pop music and films of yesteryear, especially the nineteen sixties. In all, the family agreed their diversity of age was beneficial and they were delighted when it was announced that they had come second and were awarded with a prize of twenty five pounds.

It was dark when they left the pub and walked back towards the cottage and although the rain had stopped, a misty drizzle hung in the air and there was not a breath of wind.

"Such a shame," said Lottie, looking up to the dark starless skies, as they approached the church. "There's a full moon tonight but I doubt we'll see anything of it."

"It was near enough full last night," said Zac, absently kicking a small stone as he walked along the footpath. "I woke up in the early hours and from my bedroom window looked over to the graveyard. It was really weird and creepy too. You see, I could see a dim light flashing and the shape of a figure moving around." There was a plop when the stone dropped into a drain.

"That'll be because your eyes were still sleepy," said Sandra, stifling a yawn. "A trick of the light. I've experienced things like that before."

Bill shook his head. "No, because that wouldn't explain the flashing light, would it?"

"No, no I suppose not," Sandra agreed, "but I expect there's a perfectly logical explanation."

"Well, that's as maybe," said Hetty, unnerved by the notion of strange goings-on in the graveyard, "but regrettably I can't think of one."

Kate and Vicky simultaneously glanced towards the church convinced the gargoyles on the dark tower looked even more grotesque and sinister than usual. With a shudder they linked arms and moved closer to each other.

Hetty, also feeling uncomfortable, quickened her pace. "I'm so glad our room is on the back of the cottage," she said, "and that it looks out to sea rather than over the graveyard."

Chapter Fifteen

Thursday morning was dull with a misty drizzle drifting in from the west but the forecast said that it should brighten later and so Hetty and Lottie announced during breakfast that they had decided to take a trip to St. Ives on the branch line train which ran from St. Erth.

"What about the rest of you?" Lottie asked, as she buttered a thick slice of toast. "Have you made any plans for the day?"

"Well, seeing as it's only just over two weeks now until the second series of *Poldark* starts, I think it's time I went in search of some of the locations used for filming," said Sandra. "It was high on my 'to do' list when we first arrived here but what with one thing and another it seems to have slipped right down to the bottom."

"Yes, I agree that should be interesting," said Bill, "so I shall go with you. Be nice to do a bit of sight-seeing. Have you anywhere in mind?"

"I thought Charlestown," said Sandra. "I've looked it up and it's near St. Austell."

"Good choice," said Bill, "and then afterwards we could go to visit the Eden Project. I was reading about it the other day and know it's out that way somewhere."

All three children were impressed by their parents' plans and so agreed that they would accompany them on their excursion. And to enable them to get away early, Lottie and Hetty insisted on clearing away the breakfast things and tidying up. When the chores were done, they too left the cottage. As they walked towards the bus stop, Lottie caught sight of a notice board beside the church gate. Knowing the bus wasn't due for another ten minutes she crossed the road to see if there was anything of interest coming up in the village during their stay. One notice told of Bingo evenings which occurred every Tuesday in the village hall; she thought that was worth considering but then she saw something even more interesting:

notification of a garden party at Pentrillick House on Sunday afternoon which was to be opened by Rosie Rutherford. It stated there would be something for everyone including a raffle in which one of Rosie's paintings was to be a prize. Proceeds were in aid of the local community centre which was in need of a new roof.

"Excellent," said Lottie, memorising the details so that she could pass them on to Hetty, who was patiently waiting on the other side of the road.

Once on the bus, Hetty and Lottie again sat upstairs and as the bus neared the garage both peered from the window hopeful of catching a glimpse of Vince Royale doing something incriminating. To their delight they saw him on the forecourt but his actions appeared to be perfectly innocent, for he was again talking to Alison Rowe, the pub's landlady, but this time as she filled up her car with petrol.

By the time the bus reached Penzance the mist had cleared and the sun was trying to peep through the milky white cloud but to the dismay of many, it did not succeed. However, the sisters were not to be downcast by the weather. They cheerfully alighted the bus and went into the railway station which was conveniently very close by.

After a short journey on a mainline train the sisters disembarked at the first stop, St Erth, and from there caught the branch-line train for the fifteen minute journey to St Ives.

The small seaside town, as they anticipated, was very busy. Crowds walked along the narrow streets browsing through merchandise in shops and patronising the many cafés and restaurants. On the long beaches, despite the lack of sun, families stretched out across the sand and many were in the sea.

When Lottie saw an art gallery she suggested they take a look inside. Hetty agreed, hopeful that they might see a display of Rosie's work. They were not disappointed. Rosie's paintings took pride of place on a long stretch of wall. The sisters studied each picture with interest and were especially amused by the two penguins discreetly placed on every one but always wearing different outfits.

In another gallery they looked at pottery, hopeful of seeing work by Malcolm Biggins, but to their disappointment there was none on display. Hetty enquired at the reception desk about his work and was told he had an exhibition in Penzance near to his workshop.

As they walked along the sea front, the pungent smell of fish and chips made the sisters feel hungry and as they had been on their feet for several hours, they agreed it would be nice to sit down for a while, but not indoors. They bought two portions of fish and chips in takeaway containers and then went back outside looking for a bench; they were in luck as one was vacated by a family as they neared it.

After their late lunch they continued to explore the town's quaint nooks and crannies. Hetty bought an ice cream but Lottie declined the offer as she was still feeling full after the fish and chips. As they passed a newsagent, Hetty popped inside and bought a local paper to read when they arrived back at Pentrillick.

By mid-afternoon both sisters had aching feet and were feeling weary, so they made their way back to the small station and caught the next train. At St Erth they changed for a train to Penzance and from there caught the bus back to Pentrillick.

As they stepped from the Penzance bus, they found the family had just arrived back and Bill was parking the Volvo beside Sea View Cottage.

"Perfect timing," said Bill, stepping from the car and kissing his mother and his aunt. "Who's ready for a cup of tea?"

When they went inside they found a note on the doormat from Pentrillick House Mobile Gardening Dept. which said two gardeners would be coming to tend the garden on Saturday morning unless the weather was wet. They would not disturb the family and would access the garden by way of the side gate. However, if this was inconvenient then they were asked to phone the following number to change the date.

Lottie rubbed her hands with glee. "Hopefully I shall be able to pick the brains of the gardeners and glean some useful information regarding my aspidistra."

While the adults discussed the gardeners' visit, the children switched on the television, all three eager to see how the Brownlee brothers were doing in the triathlon. They found the lads had just dismounted their cycles and were beginning the final sprint.

Bill made tea for all the adults after which they each exchanged stories of their day's activities and all agreed that it had been nice to get out and about as there was so much to see and do when in unfamiliar territory.

Meanwhile, the children cheered and clapped their hands with glee for the brothers had come in first and second in the triathlon earning Team GB two more medals.

Later, as Hetty read her local paper, Lottie, still optimistic that one day her aspidistra might flower, took the plant outside where she hoped the fresh warm air and rain forecast to fall overnight, might freshen it up and improve its appearance. She knew it was safe to do so for the plant was unlikely to attract the attention of a passing slug, as it had no flowers yet to pollinate. Knowing it would not tolerate strong sunlight, Lottie carefully placed it behind the shed in the shade and promised to take it back inside after it had had a good wash.

When she returned indoors, Hetty pointed out an article in the local paper telling of Barry's death the previous Thursday. The report clearly stated there was strong evidence to suggest it was a case of suicide. Hetty was very annoyed. "It was not suicide," she said, tossing the newspaper onto the floor.

Lottie sat down. "As I've said before I'm inclined to agree but we can't be sure, can we, Het? I mean, if it wasn't for the confusion over the name on the so-called suicide message we wouldn't have any doubt at all, would we?"

"No, but I think the police want to believe that it was suicide so they can concentrate more on the death of Faith Trethewy. I mean, that without question was a case of cold-blooded murder and they need to solve it to put people's minds at rest."

"Good point," Sandra agreed, removing her shoes and resting her feet on a cushioned footstool, "but for the sake of the community I hope you're both wrong about Barry."

Hetty obstinately shook her head. "I'm not wrong. I feel it in my bones and by hook or by crook I shall try to find out why the lad was killed and who had a motive."

Bill frowned. "And how on earth do you propose to do that? As we've already said you only know a handful of people here and not one of them seems in the slightest bit dodgy."

"By probing and asking questions," she promptly replied, "and as regards dodgy people there must be plenty around here somewhere and so to find them I shall go to the garden party at Pentrillick House on Sunday. It's the obvious place to start especially with Faith and Barry both having worked there." She gleefully rubbed her hands together. "Hopefully there will be lots of people there and we can do some serious eavesdropping."

"We?" said Lottie.

"Yes, we. You and I, Lottie, are in this together."

Chapter Sixteen

Following a night of persistent rain, Friday dawned wet but by nine o'clock the sun was shining brightly and the weather looked settled for the day. After breakfast Sandra announced that provisions were getting low and so they really needed to go shopping. The children, not keen for a trip around a supermarket, groaned, but their attitude changed when Bill suggested they go down to Land's End first and then call in at Long Rock on the way back for the necessary shopping.

Hetty and Lottie both with aching legs from walking the previous day said that they would be happy to stay at the cottage, take their ease and read. And so the family went out mid-morning leaving Lottie sitting on the settee reading one of the novels she had bought in the charity shop and Hetty with feet tucked beneath her in an armchair reading on her Kindle. However, when Hetty reached the end of a chapter, she turned off her Kindle, removed her reading glasses and laid both down on the floor. "Would you like a coffee, Lottie?"

Lottie looked up. "Yes, thank you. That would be very nice."

Hetty disappeared into the kitchen and returned soon after with two mugs of coffee, a plate of chocolate biscuits and a notebook and pen.

"I can't concentrate on my book," she said, putting down Lottie's coffee on the table by her side, "I need to make a list of possible suspects."

Lottie frowned. "Suspects?"

"Yes, suspects. People who might have murdered Faith and Barry."

"Surely you're not serious."

"Oh, but I am." She sat down and opened up the notepad. "Now, let's get some facts down. For a start, who might need money enough to murder for it?"

Lottie laid down her book and shrugged her shoulders. "How on earth am I to know that?"

"Well, yes, I admit, it's a tricky one, but you do agree that the person who shot poor Faith must have gone to her house to steal the money she had stashed away?"

Lottie hesitated with her reply. "Yes, but I thought you'd decided it was also possible that the death might have been premeditated and that the culprit was someone who knew she was there and that her car had gone in for its MOT."

Hetty scowled. "Yes, admittedly I did but on reflection I think it more likely that robbery was the real motive."

"I see."

"So, come on, Lottie, and imagine you're a private detective."

Lottie tutted. "That's an absurd idea. Anyway, surely the police will be working along the lines of a bungled burglary and they'll have a much better idea of who might be a suspect than we'd ever be able to come up with."

"That's as maybe but it doesn't mean that we can't have a go. Come on, Lottie. Put your thinking cap on and tell me what sort of person would steal money."

Lottie picked up her coffee. "Oh, well...umm...I suppose someone who was in debt might be desperate enough to risk being caught."

"Yes, yes, that's the type of person we're looking for. But I don't think it would be someone who was in trouble with say household bills, rent etc. because you can get help with things like that. I'm inclined to think the guilty person may have been say, a gambler who owes money and can't bear to tell his wife or partner."

"Oh dear, that's a horrible thought. My Hugh was dead against gambling of any sort. He wouldn't even do the National Lottery when it first came out but changed his mind after a while when he learned of some of the good causes it helped."

Hetty nodded. "Yes, your Hugh was a good sort."

Lottie's eyes half-filled with tears. "Anyway," she said, wiping her eyes on the back of her hand, "do you have any other theories as to why someone would be desperate enough to steal?"

"Oh yes, you bet I do," said Hetty, "a compulsive gambler for instance or someone who needed the money for drugs."

Lottie gasped. "But surely you don't get people like that in villages, especially in Cornwall. Drug people, I mean. Surely that's a town and city problem."

Hetty sighed. "My dear, Lottie, you are just so very naïve."

Lottie half-smiled. "Yes, I suppose I am. If the truth be known I've led a very sheltered life. Hugh took care of everything and I just did my housework, looked after the children and made cakes." She sighed. "I sometimes wish I'd had a career like you, Het. But don't get me wrong, the children were and still are my life…it's just, well…you know."

Hetty laughed. "And you've no idea how many times I've thought how nice it would have been to be a housewife like you, Lottie."

"Anyway," said Lottie, not wanting to get sentimental, "we also have to take into consideration that whoever went to steal the money *must* have known about it. They might even have known where it was kept but of course never got a chance to get to it because on the morning of the attempted robbery, poor Faith was home."

"That's a very good point. I mean, how many people would have known about it when it was news even to her own mother?"

"Perhaps, as either Maisie or Daisy suggested, she had been looking after it for someone and that someone had told someone else about it. If so the first someone, who the money belonged to, must have been someone quite close to her but he wouldn't be the person who tried to steal the money because it was his anyway."

"That sounds very confusing," said Hetty, trying to take in what her sister had said, "but I can just about see what you're getting at and of course you could well be right."

"Thank you."

Hetty rubbed her forehead as she tried to think. "But if you are right, the money must have been obtained illegally otherwise whoever it actually belonged to would have come forward before now and claimed it."

The colour drained from Lottie's face. "So, do you think the money Faith had was stolen?"

"Could be, or it might have been earned by someone who was paid in cash and didn't want to pay tax on it. On the other hand, perhaps she got it through blackmail."

"Blackmail," repeated Lottie, "whatever do you mean?"

Hetty lowered her voice even though there was no-one other than the sisters in the house. "Well, I got the impression she wasn't opposed to having a clandestine affair with married men. Therefore, might she have obtained the money through blackmailing them, her threat being she would tell their unsuspecting wives?"

Lottie was shocked. "But that's a terrible thing to suggest, Hetty. You know I'm very much against anyone speaking ill of the dead, especially when as in this case the poor woman was murdered. Please tell me you don't really believe she would be wicked enough to blackmail anyone."

"Okay, fair enough, if it upsets you that much I'll say no more and we'll not bother to surmise as to where the money came from. I suppose it doesn't matter anyway. At least not as regards our enquiries."

Lottie finished her coffee and placed the mug back on the table. "Thank you."

"Anyway," said Hetty, "at least we have a motive, so that's enough to get on with now."

Lottie smiled. "Yes, but then so do the police so really we're getting nowhere fast."

"You're right of course, but nevertheless, we must be optimistic and persevere. I think now we'll make a list of all the men we know irrespective of whether or not we think they might be guilty."

"And women," said Lottie. "Criminals are often women."

"Hmm, yes, I suppose so. We'll do the men first though. So, who shall we start with?"

"Tommy Thomas from the charity shop," said Lottie, without hesitation. "Something doesn't ring true with him."

Hetty wrote down his name. "I agree, and I think it's a bit odd that he suddenly starts chatting away in an Irish accent."

Lottie nodded. "Yes, but it has to be said that he was very convincing even if it was a bit creepy."

Hetty tapped the pen on her teeth, clearly thinking. "Someone else I think is a bit creepy is the potter chap. Trouble is I can't remember his name."

"Malcolm Biggins," said Lottie, "but I didn't think he was creepy. In fact I thought him very handsome."

"Yes well, each to their own but I thought he had a funny gait." Hetty wrote down his name.

"Don't forget Bernie the Boatman," said Lottie, "and Ashley from the pub."

Hetty added their names to the list. "And we must also include Tristan Liddicott-Treen too, although I can't see that he'd be short of money and even if he was, he'd be far too honourable to kill for it."

Lottie giggled. "I agree, but to be fair we must include everyone."

"Prince Vince from the garage," said Hetty, suddenly, "I can't believe we've not put him down yet."

"Absolutely, but I don't think he's short of a bob or two either."

"Hmm, maybe not, but we've included Tristan Liddicott-Treen so we must include Prince Vince too."

"And the owner of this cottage, Lance Tait," said Lottie, "he's another. I know he doesn't live down here but he comes down from time to time."

"True, and we really should include Doug and Don for the same reason, especially with Doug having taken a fancy to Faith. You know, it makes him a bit suspicious."

Lottie didn't look convinced but chose not to comment and instead said, "We mustn't forget the husbands of Maisie and Daisy even though I've no idea what either of them are called."

"Neither have I," said Hetty, "so I'll write them down as Mr D and Mr M. Now how many is that?" She counted up the names. "Oh dear we only have eleven and if I'm honest, I don't think any of them really seem suspicious."

"Let's do the women then."

Hetty laughed. "Well, for a start there's Daisy and Maisie."

Lottie's face reddened with embarrassment. "What would they say if they knew we'd included them on a list of suspects?"

"Hopefully, we'll never find out. Come on think of some more; my mind's gone blank."

"Samantha Liddicott-Treen and Rosie Rutherford," said Lottie. "Then there's Chloe from the café and of course her husband, Colin to go on the chaps' list." She closed her eyes to think of more. "Ah yes, Alison the pub's landlady but I daresay the police have already ruled her out and we know she has an alibi. And then of course there's Tommy Thomas' mother but we don't know her name and Bernie the Boatman's wife but we don't know her name either."

"Wow, wow, slow down," said Hetty scribbling down the names.

Lottie shook her head. "That's it. I really can't think of anyone else."

"Damn it, nor can I and of course there are dozens of people, male and female who we've never even met or heard of."

"Just remembered two more," said Lottie, "there's the woman who we saw in the charity shop who said about the money in the knicker drawer and also Tess Dobson of whom she spoke, who cleans for Rosie."

"Well remembered," said Hetty, adding the names to the list.

"What about the youngsters?" Lottie asked.

Hetty wrinkled her nose. "I think it would be silly to include them. I mean, some of them are still at school and the rest at college or university."

"Yes, but young people need money just as much as anyone else, in fact probably more, because in this day and age they're all desperate not to get left behind with all the technology stuff, most of which I know nothing about."

"You've a good point there and of course we mustn't forget that Faith's laptop and phone were stolen. Although the phone wasn't a smart phone so I daresay a young person wouldn't want to be seen dead with whatever it was."

"What about the laptop?"

Hetty put the pen and notebook down on the arm of the settee and picked up her coffee. "Not sure about that. It's a pity we don't know what type it was because if we did we could ask Zac or the girls whether or not it was desirable."

Lottie picked up a biscuit and licked the chocolate. "Hmm, anyway, at least we have a list now, albeit brief, and we have a motive. So what next?"

"I don't know, Lottie, but from now on we really must keep our ears open and our eyes peeled because when all is said and done, someone killed Faith and I'm pretty sure it was a local."

"I agree, but what about Barry?" Lottie asked.

Hetty groaned. "I think we'll leave that one for another day."

It was late afternoon when the family arrived back from their trip to Land's End laden with shopping, and as they packed it away, Bill suggested they all go to the pub again in the evening for dinner, despite the vast amount of food just purchased.

"Excellent idea," said Lottie, "I've not been out at all today and could really do with some fresh air."

Hetty groaned. "But it's Friday."

"*Gardeners' World*?" laughed Bill.

Hetty nodded.

"Well, we could always do the same as last week," said Sandra, who was keen to eat out.

"Yes, yes," said Hetty, "that's fine with me. Don't let me hold you back. I'll make myself a sandwich again."

"But you had a sandwich for lunch," said Lottie.

Hetty tutted. "Then I'll have something else. Please don't worry about me. I've hardly worked up an appetite. Like you, I've not even left the house all day."

Hetty watched *Gardeners' World*, determined that she would not let herself get into a tiswas as she had done the previous week. However, when the programme finished and she stood up to draw the curtains she felt sure that she saw someone lurking outside in the front garden hiding amongst the flowers and shrubs. Hetty sat back down, took in a deep breath and tried to keep calm and convince herself that it was a trick of the light or a reflection of something inside the room. When she eventually felt composed, she rose and with a brave face, carried her empty plate into the kitchen where she rinsed it under the tap. After placing it on the draining board, she left the kitchen and closed the door behind her. As she slipped on her jacket, she dropped her mobile phone into her pocket rather than her handbag just in case she should need to use it quickly.

The light was fading fast as she locked the front door and when she stepped onto the pavement she felt a fresh breeze blowing along the street. As she closed the garden gate she cast a glance at the shrubs but detected no movement other than the rustling of leaves caused by the wind.

Along the road, faint shadows waved beneath the lamplights, and warm glows shone out from house windows. With haste Hetty made her way to the pub but gave the house where the dog had barked the previous Friday, a very wide berth.

It was almost eleven o'clock when the family arrived back at the cottage and instantly Hetty felt ill-at-ease. The garden gate was not latched and when they went inside she saw the kitchen door was wide open.

"What's the matter, Het?" Lottie asked, seeing her sister's pale face, "you look like you've seen a ghost."

Hetty smiled weakly and nodded her head in the direction of the children. Understanding the gesture, Lottie said, "I suppose you're just tired."

Hetty forced a false yawn. "Yes, I am tired. Today seems to have been a very long one."

"And so am I," said Zac, "goodnight everyone."

Vicky and Kate likewise left for their bedroom.

"What's wrong?" Lottie asked, as soon as she heard the twins close their bedroom door.

Hetty sat down on the settee. Her hands were shaking. "Without doubt, I latched the garden gate when I left here earlier and I also closed the kitchen door," she said. "Someone has been in here prowling around."

Chapter Seventeen

Sandra woke at six o'clock on Saturday morning and quietly slipped into the en suite bathroom. Outside she could hear the rain lashing hard against the window and something blowing around in the back garden. Unable to see through the frosted glass, she opened the window. It was high tide and a huge sea was battering the shore, rattling the shingle and dragging back the sand into the frothing grey water. Along the sea front bedraggled bunting flapped and snapped in the ferocious westerly wind, and the two wooden benches dripped with the spray from the thrashing waves and the pouring rain.

In the garden below, the green plastic watering can which usually stood beside the outside tap, bounced and slid across the patio along with a lightweight dustbin lid.

Sandra sighed. A day on the beach was out of the question and so they must come up with an indoor plan for the day. Furthermore, there was little chance of the gardeners from Pentrillick House putting in an appearance either.

To avoid alarming the children, nothing was said during breakfast regarding Hetty's claim that someone had been inside the house the previous night while they were at the Crown and Anchor. Besides, after a thorough search they had found that nothing was missing nor was anything disturbed. Secretly they all thought that Hetty had not closed the kitchen door as she claimed, and as for the gate, that could have blown open in the wind if not latched properly.

After breakfast, Sandra looked on her laptop for things to do in Cornwall when the weather was bad. She found there was a skittle alley not too far away which met with the children's approval. Meanwhile, Hetty and Lottie decided they would take the bus into Helston for a look round and have lunch while they were there.

As the morning wore on, the rain began to ease but the wind continued to blow and buffet everything in its path. After the family had gone to the skittle alley, Hetty and Lottie prepared themselves for their trip into Helston. It was as Lottie buckled up her shoes that she suddenly remembered the aspidistra. She dashed outside and to her relief found that due to shelter provided by the shed it had not suffered and been battered by the wind, nor had it blown over, but it was very wet. Apologising to the plant for leaving it outside, Lottie lifted the large plastic flower pot out of the replica Victorian planter and tipped the surplus water onto the path; she then took it back indoors.

Hetty tutted as Lottie stood the plant on the draining board. "I thought you'd forgotten that thing."

Lottie took a tissue from her pocket and carefully dried the long glossy leaves. "Not likely. I'm becoming more fond of this plant every day, and even you must admit that it looks quite elegant now that it's had a good wash."

It was late-morning by the time the sisters caught the Helston bus for a journey they had established would take twenty five minutes. They sat upstairs to enjoy the view and were especially thrilled when the bus went through the village of Porthleven.

"We must come here one day," said Lottie, looking at the many boats inside the harbour wall, "it's positively bustling in spite of the weather."

Hetty agreed. "We'll come next time the sun shines. That's if it ever does."

Lottie tutted. "You should have more faith, Het. Anyway the sun will shine again. After this unsettled weekend it's looking quite promising."

The bus left Porthleven, climbed uphill and passed by the Penrose Estate. It followed the winding road which swept through woodland and over a meandering stream. As they drove into Helston Lottie pointed to ducks swimming on a small lake.

Helston was fairly quiet and as the sisters stepped from the bus a sudden sharp shower caused them to dash into the first shop they saw; to their delight, they found it was a charity shop. They stayed in the shop until the rain stopped. Hetty bought a silk scarf and Lottie bought two more books.

After walking through the town, they went into a pub for lunch and then because she was interested to see how much property cost in the area, Hetty stopped outside an estate agent's window so that she might get some idea. As she did so she heard Lottie gasp and so turned round to see the reason for her sister's exclamation.

Lottie was waving her hand and pointing her finger down the road. "Look," she said, clearly excited, "look, Het."

Hetty was nonplussed. "But I don't know what I'm looking at."

"At the bottom of the road," hissed Lottie, impatiently, "he's just going round the corner. Look, it's Tommy Thomas."

"Oh," said Hetty, frown lines forming on her brow, "I see him but I don't understand your excitement. I mean, what's so special about Tommy Thomas going round a corner?"

"It's not where he's going to but where he came from that's of interest. You wanted to know if there were any gamblers at Pentrillick, didn't you? Well there is. Tommy Thomas just came out of a betting shop."

The family were still out when Hetty and Lottie arrived back at the cottage and so they made cups of tea and drank them in the conservatory. After their cups were drained, they observed that the wind had dropped and the sun was trying to put in an appearance, and so decided to take a walk.

"Where shall we go?" Hetty asked, as they locked the front door and then walked around the back to put the key beneath the pot of marigolds.

"I rather fancy going up the lane to Blackberry Way. I liked it up there. It's away from the traffic and the view is lovely."

Hetty agreed. "Blackberry Way it is then."

The sun was rapidly drying up the road and hedgerows and were it not for the occasional puddle along the lane no-one would ever have believed the day could have begun with lashing rain and strong to gale force winds. Hetty even felt the need to unbutton her jacket due to the warmth from the sun.

Half way up the hill they saw someone walking towards them with a Yorkshire terrier on a lead. As the gap between them narrowed they realised it was Tommy Thomas from the charity shop.

When they passed him, Hetty and Lottie both said hello and Tommy returned the greeting in his near perfect Irish accent.

"What's he doing up here?" Hetty asked as she looked over her shoulder at Tommy who was walking down the hill and singing Danny Boy, "and how did he get back from Helston so quickly?"

"At a guess I'd say he's out walking his dog," said Lottie, a note of sarcasm in her voice, "and I daresay like us, he's been home for a while, especially if he drove home, which I expect he did since he wasn't on the bus."

"Yes, I suppose that's true but why come up here? I reckon he's been up to survey the scene of his crime."

Lottie shook her head and tutted. "He probably came up here for the same reason I wanted to. Because there's very little traffic and the view is lovely. Ideal for dog walking as you yourself said only the other day."

Hetty sighed. "Do you think I'm getting paranoid, Lottie?"

Lottie giggled. "At times, yes. And I really do think you should curb your suspicious nature and stop seeing everyone as a potential killer."

However, when they reached the top of the lane and turned into Blackberry Way, Lottie's suspicious nature was also aroused. For leaning on the wooden gates of Faith's house Primrose Cottage, were two dubious looking men, eagerly chatting as they gazed into Faith's front garden and pointed out various features.

Lottie and Hetty's pace slowed as they neared the two men who on realising they were not alone, ceased their loud chatter. As they walked by, both sisters were keen to note that the men had looks of guilt and embarrassment on their suntanned faces.

Chapter Eighteen

On Saturday evening, Hetty announced that she would accompany her sister, Lottie, to church the following morning having reminded Bill that he was on holiday and deserved every opportunity there was for a lie-in. Bill didn't object, although he did feel a pang of guilt on Sunday morning when he heard the sisters leaving the cottage at to quarter to nine. Needless to say, the purpose of Hetty's church attendance was not for any spiritual reason, but more the opportunity subtly to obtain information about Tommy Thomas who she now had labelled as a reckless gambler, and anyone else whom she deemed to be of dubious character. These pieces of information she proposed to acquire from either Daisy or Maisie but to her dismay, neither of the ladies was in church that morning. Furthermore, the sky was an ominous grey and the weather forecast had predicted a gloomy day, thus dampening any hopes of rooting out useful information at the Pentrillick House Garden Party to be held later.

However, Chloe from the café was in attendance with her husband, Colin, and after enquiring about the prospect of the garden party going ahead should it rain, Chloe informed the sisters that the weather would not be a problem because Tristan Liddicott-Treen had already said that if the weather was inclement then the party would go ahead as planned but in the ballroom rather than outside. Hetty left the church with a spring in her step knowing it would be far easier to eavesdrop on conversations if visitors were crammed together indoors than ever it would if they were scattered around in the extensive grounds and gardens.

When Hetty and Lottie arrived back at Sea View Cottage, the family were all in the living room. Zac looked up from his sketch pad as Lottie closed the living room door. "Did you see any weird people in the churchyard this morning?"

"Weird," repeated Hetty, sitting down to remove her shoes, "in what way weird?"

Zac screwed up his face. "I don't really know. It's just that I'm sure I saw someone in the churchyard again last night. It was dark of course but I could see a figure lurking amongst the graves and a flashing light just like before. It was quite late too. About one o'clock when I went to the bathroom for a drink of water."

Lottie sat down. "What do you mean by lurking, Zac?"

"I'm not sure, Grandma. But he appeared to be just hanging around and then he suddenly disappeared from view. Sadly I couldn't see where he went because of the trees."

"And was it just the one person?" Bill asked.

"Yes, as far as I could see."

"Probably some poor person who is homeless and sleeps in the churchyard at night," said Vicky, with a deep sigh, "there are homeless people everywhere."

"Oh no, that's a horrid thought," said Kate, "I do hope it's not true."

Zac shook his head. "I doubt it because if I were homeless and lived in Pentrillick then I'd opt for sleeping on the beach rather than the churchyard with all the spooks."

"Homeless people don't *live* anywhere, you numpty," said Vicky indignantly.

Zac tutted. "Don't be so pernickety, Vic, you know just what I mean."

"More likely to be a drunk staggering home from the pub," said Sandra, not wanting the children to squabble, "you'll probably find there's a short cut through the churchyard to somewhere or other."

Hetty shuddered. "Ugh, you wouldn't catch me going through the churchyard in the middle of the night, sober or drunk."

Vicky and Kate promptly cheered up and giggled. Their imaginations fired up by the vision of a drunken great aunt.

After lunch, having spent the morning doing very little, some family members changed their clothes in preparation for the Garden Party. Sandra was the first to be ready and so she washed up, and afterwards reluctantly discarded the flowers which they had received from Rosie Rutherford with compliments from Lance Tait on the day they had arrived. It saddened her to throw them away but they really had long passed their best, especially the roses, for on each stem very few petals remained. Sandra sighed, already two weeks of the holiday had gone, and in half that time again they would be on their way home.

Hetty and Lottie had originally planned to go to Pentrillick House for the Garden Party by means of two of the bicycles they'd found in the shed, thus saving either Bill or Sandra the bother of making two trips. However, because it was drizzling and Pentrillick House was quite a long ride from the cottage, Bill said cycling was out of the question and insisted he first take up Sandra and the girls and then come back for the ladies and Zac.

The car park was almost full when Hetty and Lottie arrived at Pentrillick House with Bill and Zac, and to Hetty's delight she observed several familiar faces amongst the considerable crowd viewing the stalls in the vestibule. As prearranged, they met up with the rest of the family in front of a grandfather clock which told the correct time and stood at the bottom of a magnificent sweeping staircase.

Beside open double doors which led into the ballroom, Rosie Rutherford manned the raffle from behind a table laden with dozens of donated prizes including one of her own paintings called *Sunset over Lizard Point* which temporarily hung on the wall behind her. She greeted the family when they bought tickets and asked if it was their first visit to Pentrillick House.

"It is for me," said Bill, folding the tickets and placing them in his wallet, "but the ladies have been once before."

Rosie smiled as she glanced towards the sisters and Sandra. "And I hope you came on a fine day."

"We did," said Sandra. "It was a beautiful day but I must say the weather this weekend has been a bit of a let-down, but we mustn't grumble."

Rosie sighed. "Yes, it's such a shame that we've had to hold this party inside. I know Tristan is really disappointed, bless him. Events such as this when forced indoors never raise as much money as when held out in the open."

"Oh dear, that is a pity," said Lottie, "We shall have to buy lots of things to help make up for the loss, providing they're not too bulky of course."

Rosie giggled. "Talking of bulky things, how is the aspidistra faring?"

"It's doing very nicely, thank you. I put it outside for a while to freshen it up and I think it's done it the world of good."

Hetty snorted but managed to refrain from making a derisory comment.

"Well, there's a plant and vegetable stall here if you're interested," said Rosie, "although I think most of the offerings are pretty common. You know, fuchsias, geraniums and suchlike."

"Really, then we shall have a look," said Sandra, "I'm very fond of fuchsias, especially if they're named varieties, but either way there's bound to be one or two I don't have at home."

Hetty held back when the rest of the family walked away to browse the other stalls. "It's probably a silly question," she whispered to Rosie, "but I'm curious to know if anyone in the village has a set of keys to our cottage?"

Rosie shook her head. "Not to my knowledge. The cleaner doesn't because she uses the ones always left under the pot of marigolds the same as you use. Obviously Lance has a set but he doesn't live in the village."

Hetty slumped her shoulders. "Oh."

"May I ask why you're curious?" Rosie said, clearly baffled.

"Oh, it's just me being silly," said Hetty, trying not to frown. "The thing is, I'm sure that before I went to the pub the other night I closed the kitchen door, but when we came back it was wide open. Not only that, when I went to close the curtains before I got ready to go out, I felt sure that I saw someone lurking in the front garden."

Rosie looked alarmed. "Really? That's a little disconcerting. Did anyone else in your family see anything?"

"The rest of us weren't there," said Lottie, who was waiting for Hetty, "because we went to the pub earlier in the evening leaving Het to join us later. She wanted to watch *Gardeners' World*, you see. That's why she felt sure she'd shut the door. No-one else was with her and so she locked up on her own."

"That's right," said Hetty, "I also closed and latched the front gate when I went and that too was open when we came back. But there was no sign of a break-in so I figured that if anyone had been in the cottage then they must have had a key."

Rosie frowned, clearly thinking hard. "Oh, I see. Well as I say, as far as I know no-one else has keys and that must be the case because only the cleaner would need to get in anyway."

Hetty's face brightened. "Good, that's made me feel a whole lot better. I suppose deep down I knew I must have been mistaken because nothing was taken or even disturbed. Thank you, Rosie: you've put my mind at rest."

Rosie smiled sweetly. "I'm glad to have been able to help. That can be my good deed for the day."

On leaving the vestibule the family went into the ballroom but because it was very crowded they decided it would be easier to get around if they split up into groups, and so the children went off on their own as did Sandra and Bill. Likewise, Hetty and Lottie with arms linked so they didn't get separated, disappeared into the crowd where they browsed the stalls and played a few games.

They were especially drawn to 'guess the weight of the cake' a seemingly popular attraction, judging by the long line of ladies in the queue, occasioned no doubt by the stall's purveyor, Tristan Liddicott-Treen. Here the two sisters, mesmerised by the host's dashing good looks and cultured voice, lingered for twenty minutes, each making seven predictions as to the weight of the rich fruit cake.

As they left Tristan Liddicott-Treen to the rest of his admirers, they saw a notice indicating cream teas. Feeling peckish, they followed a series of arrows into an adjoining room where Maisie, Daisy and Samantha Liddicott-Treen, were pouring tea and filling scones with cream and jam for a queue of a dozen or so people.

Hetty and Lottie joined the queue. Hetty wanted to ask questions about Tommy Thomas and gambling but of course the presence of others, and especially Samantha, made the subject quite impossible. However, they did learn that the following day Barry's funeral was to take place at the church.

"I think we should go," said Hetty, as she and Lottie sat down at a table with their cream teas. "I like Louise and I know you do too. It would be nice to be there and offer a bit of support. You know, let her see that people, even relative strangers like us, care."

"Yes, you're probably right but I hope you're not thinking of looking for a likely murderer amongst the mourners. I know that the police often observe funerals looking for possible suspects but from our point of view it would be most inappropriate."

Hetty shook her head. "No, Lottie, I won't be doing that. I've given a lot of thought to Barry's death and I'm inclined to think that Louise's concern over the name Baz is unfounded and it was just a careless error on his part. Much better for the lad to have taken his own life than for someone to have ended it for him."

"I agree, and there's no evidence at all to suggest Barry had any enemies anyway. In fact I'd say that he was very popular."

"Hmm, I'm sure you're right."

However, a little later they began to have their doubts.

At five o'clock the raffle was drawn and the star prize, Rosie's painting, *Sunset over Lizard Point*, was won by Faith's mother, Mrs Trethewy. Receiving the painting made her cry and the sisters were touched by her emotion. After all the other raffle prizes were drawn, they went to speak to her.

"Faith liked to paint when she was young," said Mrs Trethewy, placing the painting alongside her chair. "She liked to paint flowers, animals and birds and was actually quite good. She would have been really chuffed to know that I'd won this because she very much admired Rosie's work."

"We were told that she worked here at Pentrillick House," said Lottie, sitting down beside Mrs Trethewy, "and that she loved her job."

"Oh, she did and now poor Barry's gone too." She sighed deeply. "Faith and Barry were very good friends, you see. Barry had worked at the house ever since he'd left school. Faith was very good to him when he lost his father. Dear, dear, it was all so sad. But Faith helped him a lot. She listened to him and because he loved the gardens here she encouraged him to study horticulture. And then a few years later, after poor Faith had to give up work because of the terrible accident, Barry became a regular visitor to her place. He did all sorts of odd jobs around her house and in her garden. You know, things a bad back prevent you from doing. He seemed happy to be able to reciprocate the kindness she had shown to him." Tears welled in the eyes of Mrs Trethewy. "And now they're both gone. My only comfort is to think that they've found each other in the hereafter and so they're not alone."

After the raffle, the table was dismantled on which the prizes had been displayed and several other empty stalls were likewise cleared and whisked away to be stacked by the door ready to be returned to the community centre. Meanwhile, in the ballroom, ladies patiently gathered around the 'guess the weight of the cake' stall, to hear whose estimate had been the nearest to the correct weight. To Lottie's immense delight she was spot-on and was awarded the cake as a prize from Tristen Liddicott-Treen himself.

As the ballroom was being cleared, Lottie observed the arrival of Ashley and Alison Rowe, no doubt having just finished the Sunday lunchtime session at the Crown and Anchor. After chatting briefly with the Liddicott-Treens, both helped volunteers to arrange a dozen chairs in a semi-circle at the far end of the room in front of three tall mullioned windows. Once done, a local brass band took up their places to entertain the crowd. Had the event been held outdoors as planned then the band's requirement would have been to provide background music, but since all were confined indoors, couples took to the dance floor and for the first time in many years the ballroom was used for its original purpose.

By early evening the drizzle had diminished and so Lottie and Hetty, keen to get some fresh air went outside and while leaning on a wall which edged the steps leading up to the main door of the house, pondered over the possibility that Pentrillick House might in some way hold a link between Barry and Faith's deaths as both had worked there.

"I wish they were doing tours of the house today," said Hetty, looking up at the building towering above them, "but I can understand why they aren't. Anyway, we must come up another day to do some serious investigating because I'm itching to have a good poke round inside."

Lottie was amused by her sister's lack of reality. "I don't think there will be much of an opportunity to have a poke round, Het. Tour the house, yes, but we'll not be able to see anything they don't want us to see."

"Yes, I suppose not. Come on, let's go back inside: it feels quite chilly out here in the damp air."

But as they turned towards the door, they heard voices coming from the other side of the wall. They crossed the steps and peered to a gravelled area below. To their surprise Alison, the pub's landlady was quietly chatting to the Prince Charles lookalike, Vince Royale.

Lottie scowled. "I've a sneaky feeling there's something going on between those two. I wish I were a butterfly then I could flutter down to discover the subject of their tête-à-tête."

"Butterflies don't flutter around in damp weather, Lottie, so I think you'd have to be a fly. Having said that, you don't see many flies either when it's wet, do you?"

Lottie frowned. "You're getting very awkward in your old age, Het."

"Old age! But I'm the same age as you."

Lottie shook her head. "No, I'm ten minutes younger and that ten minutes clearly makes all the difference!"

Back inside the ballroom, couples were still dancing and so Lottie and Hetty agreed it would be nice to sit down and watch the activities. As they glanced around the room, hoping to see a couple of vacant chairs, they noticed Bill beckoning them over to where he stood. Keen to see what he wanted they made their way towards him.

"I've just been chatting to Bernie," said Bill, as they reached his side, "and knowing that you're both attempting to solve Pentrillick's murder case or cases even, I thought you'd like to know what I've just found out."

"Really, and what's that?" Lottie asked, oblivious of the amused tone of her son's voice.

"Look over there," he said with a nod of his head, "at those two men by the door talking to Tristan Liddicott-Treen. The chap with no hair is Doug and the dark-haired bloke with a beard is Don. You know, the two chaps who stayed at our cottage last winter."

The jaws of Lottie and Hetty dropped simultaneously. For the two men were the pair they had seen leaning on the gates of Faith's cottage in Blackberry Way the previous day.

Chapter Nineteen

Lottie woke early on Monday just as dawn was breaking. Eager to know the exact time she propped herself up on her elbow and looked at her watch which lay on the bedside table. It was five minutes past six. Glad that she need not get up for at least another hour she laid down her watch and prepared to snuggle back beneath the bedclothes; at the same time she glanced out of the window. Feeling it must be a trick of the light, she rubbed her eyes and moved closer to the glass. She gasped, for without doubt someone was in the back garden. Lottie sat up straight and reached for her glasses hoping they might help her to identify the intruder, but she was still none the wiser. The mystery person was of normal build and wore a hooded top. Lottie watched as the stranger walked along the garden path and then out through the back gate which led down the steps and onto the beach. She sighed as he disappeared from view. He could have been anyone.

Zac was the last down for breakfast because he had stayed up late to watch the closing ceremony of the Olympic Games.

"I can't believe that we came second on the medals' table," he said, as he sat down at the table with a mug of coffee he had just made. "I mean, we did better than in London and no-one expected that. What an achievement. I wish I'd got into a sport when I was younger."

Hetty roared with laughter. "Younger. But you're only sixteen now."

Lottie nodded. "Absolutely, and so there's no time like the present, young man."

Zac stifled a yawn. "Yes, but for most sports you need to start when you're really, really young. You know, for things like swimming, gymnastics and tennis."

"So what would you do if you could turn back the clock?" Sandra asked, amused, knowing Zac to be the least active of their three children.

"Diving, I think," said Zac, "or possibly gymnastics."

Bill laughed. "You'd not be much good at diving, son, since you don't have a head for heights."

"Yeah, I know. Oh, well, it's not going to happen anyway, is it?"

"I can't wait till the Tokyo Games," said Vicky, pouring herself a glass of orange juice, "I mean, it'll be fantastic to have surfing included."

"And skateboarding, karate, climbing and baseball," said Zac. "Roll on 2020."

Hetty frowned. "Wow! Steady on there. Good heavens, in 2020 your grandmother and I will be sixty eight. Don't wish that on us older folks just yet."

Lottie's mouth turned upside-down. "What a miserable thought."

Just before eleven o'clock, Hetty and Lottie left the cottage to attend Barry's funeral. Along one side of the road, cars were tightly parked close to each other. Inside the church every seat was taken and so they joined others standing at the back in front of the door leading into the belfry.

It was not possible to identify many people when only the backs of their heads were visible but Hetty did spot the Liddicott-Treens sitting towards the front of the church. She nodded to seal her approval, pleased to see that the family had put in an appearance. Barry had after all been one of their employees and by all accounts a loyal and hardworking employee to boot.

During the service several people spoke of their love and admiration for Barry, each one reading from carefully edited notes and attempting to amuse and tell the worth of someone they had cherished but had lost. One such person was Malcolm Biggins; he told of his first encounter with Barry who was then a teenager and how they had formed a bond over the years during which he had promised that he would never attempt to take the place of Barry's late father. Malcolm then spoke of Louise, Barry's mother, his dear beloved partner and he recounted stories told to him by Louise of

Barry's first years, his first step, his first words, his first day at school and his childhood antics.

After the service everyone filed outside the church for the interment: many deep in thought, some tearful, and all moved by the affectionate sentiments expressed from the pulpit and the choice of emotional music.

Lottie and Hetty, stood well back and away from close family and friends as people gathered near to the freshly dug grave. Many of the mourners were young and they stood huddled close together. Amongst them was Emma from the café, her eyes red from crying. Hetty glanced around, half expecting to see Doug and Don even though there was no obvious reason for them be in attendance. She was relieved to see they were not there. However, amongst the mourners Lottie did spot Maisie and Daisy, but for reasons of courtesy neither she nor Hetty made any attempt to attract their attention.

After the interment, people left the churchyard and slowly made their way along the road to the Crown and Anchor for refreshments. When Daisy spotted the sisters, she waved and then with Maisie crossed over to where Hetty and Lottie stood beside the wall.

"How sweet of you to come," said Maisie, pushing a damp tissue into her handbag. "I'm sure Louise will be very moved by the large turnout."

"We both agreed that we had to come and pay our respects," said Hetty. "I know we didn't know Barry but for some reason we feel that we did, if that makes sense."

Daisy nodded. "Yes, I think I know what you mean."

"We've known Barry since the day he was born," said Maisie. "Poor lad, poor, poor lad."

"Of course," said Lottie, "it must a very, very sad day for all of you."

"I'm so glad to see that Alfie was able to make it," said Maisie, "I know he's been a bit under the weather since he had to have his appendix out."

Daisy noticed the inquisitive frown on Hetty's face. "Alfie is Chloe's little brother. He and Barry were good friends. They are both gardeners, you see. Or should I say was in Barry's case. That's him over there with Chloe and Colin and the young lady with him is his wife. She's a receptionist at the Pentrillick Hotel."

Hetty nodded. "Ah, now you come to mention it, I can see a likeness between Chloe and her brother. I take it the café is closed today then."

"Oh, yes. Chloe said she wouldn't work and didn't expect her girls to either as they were friends of Barry's."

"We weren't sure whether or not you'd be here," said Hetty, "it being your day in the charity shop."

Daisy moved aside to allow a wheelchair to pass by. "We've closed the shop but only for the morning. At first Tommy was going to cover for us but then he remembered that his old mother had a hospital appointment today and so he's had to take her to that."

Hearing mention of Tommy caused Hetty to remember the betting shop incident but she said nothing as a funeral seemed neither the time nor the place.

"Are you coming along with us to the pub?" Daisy asked, watching the last of the mourners leave the churchyard.

Hetty and Lottie simultaneously shook their heads. "No, no that's for you local folks," said Hetty. "We shall return to the cottage now to see what the rest of the family are up to."

"I see, well we won't be there long ourselves as we're opening up the shop at one," said Maisie. "Got to take the money when we can and there are lots of holiday makers still around this week."

As they left the church, Hetty suggested to Lottie that it might be a good idea, as the weather was fine, to visit Pentrillick House in the afternoon and take a guided tour of the inside rooms and Lottie agreed. When they arrived back at the cottage they found the Volvo was gone and all the family were out, except Zac, who was in the kitchen drinking coffee.

"Have they all gone out and left you alone?" Lottie asked, dropping her handbag onto the work surface.

"Yes and no," said Zac, draining his coffee mug. "They've all gone to Falmouth to have a look round, but I didn't want to go. I'm off out kayaking in a minute, you see, with Kyle and some of the others. Kyle said he would call for me after he's changed - he having been to Barry's funeral this morning."

"Yes, we saw a lot of young people there," said Lottie, "but aren't they going to join everyone else in the pub?"

Zac shook his head. "No, they said they wanted to feel close to Barry and Barry being the outdoor type, they'd feel he was with them more if they were out in the kayaks."

"That's a nice thought," said Lottie, "a very nice thought."

"So if Kyle was at the funeral, who delivered the bread today?" Hetty asked.

"No-one," said Zac, "everyone on the round was told well in advance there would be no delivery on the day of Barry's funeral. Everyone who works at Pentrillick House has the day off, you see, so that they could all attend."

"Everyone," repeated Hetty, "so does that mean the house is not open today?"

Zac nodded. "Yep."

After Zac left the cottage, the sisters made themselves some lunch and as they ate their sandwiches in the conservatory, Lottie told Hetty that she had seen someone in the back garden early that morning.

Hetty was dumbfounded. "Why on earth haven't you said anything before now?" she asked.

"Because I've been trying to convince myself that I was mistaken. You know, trick of the light or something like that. But deep down I know there really was somebody there, although no doubt there's a perfectly innocent explanation."

"Such as?"

"What? Oh...umm," playing for time, Lottie took a bite of her sandwich. "I expect it was someone out for an early morning stroll who nipped into the garden for a quick look round."

"An early morning stroll when it's barely light. Come on, Lottie, that's a bit far-fetched."

"Well can you come up with a better reason?"

Hetty nodded. "Absolutely, you bet I can. It'll be the same person who got inside the house last Friday and left the kitchen door open when we were all at the pub."

"But I thought we'd agreed that you were mistaken about that."

"Well I've changed my mind."

"But that's silly because even if someone had been in the house it doesn't mean they'd have a reason to be out in the garden as well, does it?"

Hetty sighed. "No, I suppose not, unless someone was poking around to scare us because they think we're on to them."

Lottie threw back her head and laughed. "Really, that's absurd, because we're not, are we?"

Hetty smiled. "Regrettably not."

After lunch, both feeling disappointed that a visit to Pentrillick House was not possible the sisters turned over other ways of spending the afternoon. After much deliberation they decided to stay in the village and visit the charity shop where Lottie hoped to purchase a coat or a jacket. This was because the weather had been warm and sunny when Lottie left her home for the holiday and the only jacket she had packed was lightweight and thin, hence, in the evenings when they went to the pub and it felt a little chilly, she often complained that she was feeling cold. She didn't want to buy a new coat as she had several back home, therefore as a stopgap, to buy one from the charity shop seemed the ideal solution.

To her delight, she found a warm jacket which smelled fresh and looked clean in a colour she liked which also suited her. It appeared to be in very good condition except for a small hole inside the pocket where the seam had come undone. But as this wouldn't be visible she considered it didn't matter, besides, she would mend it when she got home if she chose to keep it.

As Lottie was paying for the coat, she casually mentioned the early morning prowler. Maisie was nonplussed. "How odd. Was it a man or a woman?" she asked, as she slipped the coat into a carrier bag.

Lottie shook her head. "It was barely light and he or she wore a hooded top, so regrettably I've no idea."

"Probably a beach-comber," said Daisy, dusting and re-arranging books on a shelf, "and he took a short cut through Sea View's garden to get to the beach."

Maisie nodded. "Yes, most likely, it's quite a hobby with some people around here as you never know what'll have been washed up in the hours of darkness." She laughed. "Lots of people have found pieces of Lego."

"Lego," repeated Lottie.

"Yes, a container full of Lego fell into the sea in 1997," said Maisie, "and even today pieces regularly get washed up on both the north and the south coast."

"Really," said Hetty, how weird. But putting Lego to one side for a moment, surely beachcombers wouldn't go through our garden. I mean, that would be trespassing."

"Yes, it would," said Daisy, dropping a book with loose pages into a box, "but for much of the year the cottage is empty so they'd never be seen and even if they were seen when it's occupied they'd know that holiday makers are unlikely to do anything about it."

Lottie sighed. "No, I suppose not. At least you've put my mind at rest."

Daisy, having finished re-arranging the books, returned to the counter. "You know Tommy, the chap who works here?" she said.

Hetty and Lottie both nodded. "Well, he often goes out beachcombing although I must admit it's mostly in the winter when the seas are rougher." She wrinkled her nose. "Having said that, he would never go through your garden because it would take him out of his way."

Hearing mention of Tommy caused Hetty's face to light up. "We think we saw your Tommy in Helston the other day. Does he work there?"

"Hmm, he might have been working there but I doubt it," said Maisie, with a gentle shake of her head, "I think most of his round is out this way."

"Round?" Hetty repeated, nonplussed.

"Yes, he's a window cleaner," said Daisy, amused by Hetty's puzzled expression, "mind you I don't think he works a day more than he needs."

Maisie agreed. "He lives with his mum, you see, and she owns the house so his living expenses don't amount to a great deal as I'm pretty sure Mrs Thomas pays most of the bills."

"A window cleaner," said Hetty, "well I never. You don't come across many of them these days. I wonder why not. I can't remember the last time I saw one at work. Can you, Lottie?"

Lottie shook her head.

"Actually, to be fair to Tommy, one of his clients is Tristan Liddicott-Treen," said Maisie, "and I reckon it'd be a good day's work to get all those windows cleaned. I've never counted them but there must be dozens."

The family arrived back from their trip to Falmouth shortly after the sisters returned from the charity shop. They said they'd had a very interesting day walking the streets of the coastal town, browsing the shops and then rounding off the day with a visit to Pendennis Castle.

"A castle," said Hetty, moving her handbag off the settee so that Sandra could sit down, "how lovely, that would have been fascinating. I didn't even know there was one in Falmouth."

"There's one near here too," said Vicky, "I was reading about it the other day. It's called Pengersick Castle and it's supposed to be haunted."

Hetty laughed. "I think you'll find most castles claim to have at least one ghost."

Seeing Sandra and Bill both looked weary as they sat side by side on the settee, Lottie insisted on making mugs of tea for everyone and cutting each a generous slice of the cake she had won for guessing its weight at the garden party.

"How are your murder investigations going?" Bill asked, his tongue firmly in his cheek.

"Not very well," sighed Hetty, oblivious of his ridicule, "but we shall persevere."

Bill tutted. "Oh dear, and you don't have much time left now as we go home on Saturday."

Lottie smiled. "Probably just as well."

Zac arrived back at the cottage in the early evening, his face flushed and his hair damp.

"Did you have a good day?" Sandra asked, as he dropped wearily down into one of the armchairs.

"Absolutely fantastic," he said, "I never dreamt kayaking could be such fun or such hard work. There are lots of caves along the shore that you can't see from the beaches and coastal paths. We've been looking inside some of them. They're really creepy and made me think of smugglers and stuff like that."

"Wow," said Vicky, "it'd be brill if smugglers were still around today."

"Regrettably they are," said Hetty, "but sadly today their illicit cargo is likely to be people, firearms or drugs. Not quite as romantic as French brandy, china, perfume and silk."

"Ugh, I didn't think of that," said Vicky. "People smuggling and stuff like that is gross."

"How many of you went?" Bill asked.

"Five," said Zac. "I went in the two seater with Kyle because I'd not been kayaking before but the others were all in singles."

"Did any of your new friends go to Barry's funeral this morning?" Sandra asked. "Other than Kyle, that is."

"Yes, they all went and so were a bit low when we first met up which is hardly surprising. They soon perked up though when we got in the water, even Emma who was crying when we met her on the beach."

Sandra tutted. "Poor things. It's bad enough coping with death when you're older but for youngsters it must be very difficult. Especially when the deceased is one of your own."

Zac removed his trainers as they were a little damp. "Yes, and Emma told me that she was surprised and rather annoyed by Malcolm Biggins' funeral speech. Barry wasn't very keen on him, you see, because apparently Biggins was always suggesting Barry try to find himself a nice little wife and get settled down. Poor Barry felt the potter wanted him out of the way and so he spent as little time as possible at home."

Hetty and Lottie exchanged looks of surprise but neither chose to comment on Zac's revelation. Instead, Lottie fetched her new coat from the bedroom and modelled it for the family to see.

Once Zac had showered and changed, they all left the cottage for dinner at the Crown and Anchor. It was a chilly evening and so Lottie wore her newly acquired jacket, which had the family's approval. To her surprise, Daisy from the charity shop was in the pub with her husband who was celebrating his sixty sixth birthday.

"It looks really nice on you," Daisy said to Lottie in hushed tones so that others might not hear when they bumped into each other in the Ladies. "Might be worth a few bob one day too because it used to belong to Rosie Rutherford."

Lottie was delighted. "Really, had you not told me that I should probably have passed it on to a charity shop when I got back home, but I won't now."

Daisy took a comb from her handbag. "Yes, Rosie often brings in bags of clothes. She does a lot for the village one way or another." She lifted up her right foot. "These shoes were hers. I'm dead chuffed that we have the same size feet."

As Lottie and Daisy left the Ladies, Lottie saw Vince Royale enter the bar through the back door and as he passed by Alison who was collecting empty glasses he gave her a quick peck on the cheek. Daisy appeared not to notice but Lottie was baffled and promptly decided there was definitely something going on between Vince Royale and Alison Rowe.

Chapter Twenty

On Tuesday morning Lottie and Hetty made preparations for their third visit to Pentrillick House with every intention of looking for clues, no matter how small, which might point them in the direction of anyone who could have had a reason to murder Faith, the estate's erstwhile manager. Because the weather was glorious they decided to ride up on the bicycles they had found in the garden shed on their arrival, even though neither sister had ridden a bicycle within the past thirty years.

After making sure there were no spiders or any other creepy-crawlies hiding on the dusty bicycle frames, Lottie and Hetty left the cottage in very high spirits. As they peddled through the village, they discussed observations they'd made the previous evening while sitting in their respective beds propped up with pillows and sipping mugs of frothy drinking chocolate. They had chatted until way past the midnight hour; the subject of their conversation was of course Faith and her mysterious death and both agreed that without doubt any evidence regarding her demise, and even that of Barry Pascoe too, must surely be found at the home of the Liddicott-Treens. And they considered that having learned Tommy Thomas was a window cleaner who had the contract for cleaning the windows of Pentrillick House certainly justified the dubious title Hetty had awarded him of Suspect Number One. Although it has to be said that neither sister chose for one moment to contemplate where a humble Cornish window cleaner might have acquired the gun used in the robbery that went so very wrong.

After walking around the grounds of the house, admiring a bed crammed with blue and white agapanthus and talking to the gardeners on the off chance they might glean some useful facts and information, the sisters booked themselves places for a tour of the house and then walked through the avenue of trees and down to the café. The sun was shining and so they took mugs of steaming coffee over the lawns to the water's edge and there sat down on a bench beside a huge clump of pampas grass.

Hetty and Lottie sipped their drinks in silence and watched swans causing ripples in the water as they gracefully swam towards the middle of the vast lake, where two weeping willow trees and various colourful shrubs grew densely on the small round island. Further along, a family of ducks swam near to the water's edge, and on the path which ran round the lake, two seagulls were fighting over chips dropped by a passing visitor.

"I think we ought not to lose sight of the fact that according to Zac's new friends, Malcolm Biggins the potter and Barry didn't seem to get along too well," said Hetty, as she finished her coffee, "even though I have to admit his eulogy yesterday was very convincing."

Lottie nodded. "Yes, it was, which makes it difficult to know who to believe."

Hetty laid her empty mug down on the arm of the bench. "I agree and deep down I want to believe that Barry's death was suicide but every now and then I can't help but feel there is justified reason to doubt it."

"Yes, similar thoughts frequently cross my mind but I don't think we should jump to any conclusions without concrete evidence." Lottie chuckled. "And to be fair, I think we're probably on a wild goose chase trying to pin Faith's murder on Tommy Thomas. I mean, what evidence exactly do we have against him?"

Hetty thought for a moment. "Well, umm, very little other than we think he might have needed Faith's money to aid a gambling problem."

"Exactly," laughed Lottie, "and we don't even know that he has a gambling problem. What's more, the fact he cleans the windows here is absolutely irrelevant. Anyway, how would he know about Faith's money when even her own mother was unaware of it?"

"I don't know but it's fun to speculate," said Hetty, "and it's adding a bit of excitement to the holiday."

"It's certainly doing that. My brain is working overtime. I shall be lost when we get back home."

As they stood up to leave, the colour suddenly drained from Hetty's face and she quickly sat back down on the bench.

"What's the matter, Het? You look awful."

"It just suddenly came to me, Lottie. How Tommy could have known about the money, I mean. He's a window cleaner, isn't he? So one day he could have been up a ladder cleaning Faith's bedroom window and seen her inside the room counting out all those twenty pound notes."

Lottie sat back down too. "That's a horrible thought, Het, but it's more than possible. Oh dear, I've gone all goose pimply." She rubbed her arms. "So now I suppose we need to find out if he ever cleaned Faith's windows."

"Well, that shouldn't be too difficult."

"No, it shouldn't, but I hope that he didn't."

Hetty bit her bottom lip. "So do I."

Once the sisters felt composed they walked up towards the house in order to join the last conducted tour of the day. Inside the large vestibule, a dozen or so people were already assembled and as the grandfather clock by the foot of the stairs struck four, their guide, a short stocky man who introduced himself as Christopher appeared from an adjoining room. Once Christopher had checked off the names on his tour list, he led the party up the curved grand staircase to view the rooms set aside for the public eye. The bedrooms, clearly for show and never used, were magnificent, each with a four poster bed and breath-taking views looking down through the avenue of trees towards the lake. The sisters followed the others in the group from room to room and along creaking panelled hallways lined with old paintings, many of Liddicott-Treens from years gone by. After the bedrooms they went up a small flight of stairs to the servants' quarters and a nursery, fully equipped with a cradle, a bed, table and chairs, a tall boy and an old wooden rocking chair. Scattered over the floor were old-fashioned toys and in a corner stood a dappled rocking horse. The sun was streaming in through a south facing window and glimpses of the sea were visible in the distance over the tree tops. From a window on the western side, the famous maze formed a backdrop to the colourful rose garden. Hetty and Lottie wondered if anyone was inside the maze struggling to find a way out. It was not possible to see for the hedges were extremely tall.

Once the tour of the upstairs rooms was complete they made their way down yet another staircase and into the original kitchen which was no longer in use. Standing on the cold flagstone floor, they gazed at the huge inglenook fireplace and the ancient ovens by which stood a lone Windsor chair. A large wooden table dominated the middle of the room and a dresser decked with crockery reached from floor to ceiling. From hooks across the full lengths of the old wooden beams, brightly polished copper pots and pans, reflected the faces of the touring party.

Through a door leading into an adjoining room, two huge sinks stood alongside shelves laden with platters and earthenware dishes in all shapes and sizes.

After the kitchen and scullery they toured the dining room, oblong in shape and with a long, highly polished, mahogany table in the centre with places lavishly laid for eighteen people. Above the table, a crystal chandelier sparkled in a beam of sunlight and above the fireplace hung the portrait of an elderly gentleman whose expression seemed to ooze disapproval regarding strangers intruding into his space. Reception rooms followed and then a wide corridor. As they passed a large window, Lottie paused to touch and admire the heavy brocade curtains.

"They must weigh a ton," she said to Hetty who was in front of her.

Hetty glanced back. "Hmm, and I daresay they're full of dust and nasty little dust mites. I mean, you can't just bung something like that in the washing machine, can you?"

Lottie smiled. "Trust you to think of that." She turned to walk on but then suddenly gasped and tugged at Hetty's sleeve to pull her back. For on the wooden sill, part-hidden between one of the curtains and a large flower arrangement, lay a small hand gun.

Hetty and Lottie both stopped walking, their faces were white and they both felt cold, but before they had a chance to take a closer look, Christopher the guide beckoned them on to catch up with the rest of the group. The sisters did as they were asked and followed Christopher and the party into another room which was a library.

"We'll pop back after the tour," whispered Hetty, annoyed that they'd lost the chance for a closer look. "I'm sure no-one will notice if we do."

But to their dismay, they learned they would be unable to retrace their steps, for the house was closed up after the tour and everyone was asked to vacate the building.

In the evening, Lottie and Hetty casually declared that they'd decided to go along to the village hall for a game or two of bingo. They made the announcement with bated breath, desperately hoping that no other family members would think it a good idea and say that they would join them. They were lucky: having spent the morning on the beach and the afternoon walking the coastal path the family were all feeling tired and finding it hard to keep awake.

The reason for the sisters' apprehension was that they were not going to play bingo at all. Their plan was to return to Pentrillick House and then as the light was beginning to fade, to gain access to the grounds and enter the house by some means in order to track down the gun they had seen earlier in the day during the guided tour.

According to the notice beside the church gate, bingo began at eight o'clock and so the sisters, both dressed in black, said goodbye to the family at a quarter to eight and left by the front door. After closing the garden gate they slipped around to the side of the house where they had left the bicycles leaning on the gable wall of the cottage. Feeling like naughty children they climbed on the bicycles and peddled off as quickly as their aged legs would permit.

It was half past eight and the sun was rapidly setting when the boundary walls of Pentrillick House came into view. Fully aware that they couldn't enter the estate by the main entrance, Hetty and Lottie cycled around the wall looking for a low part over which they might be able to climb. They were in luck. Beneath a densely wooded area, part of the wall had tumbled down thus giving them not only a way of entry into the grounds but also cover under which to hide their bicycles.

Once over the wall they rested on the trunk of a fallen tree and waited until lights came on in various parts of the house and curtains were drawn across the windows. They then ran beneath the trees and across the lawns to the back of the house where they hid behind a tall yew hedge to rest again and get back their breath. Once their thumping hearts had returned to a normal rhythm, they slowly approached the house, praying the Liddicott-Treens had no dogs, or if they did that they were sound asleep indoors.

Keeping close to the wall, they edged their way along the back of the house desperately hoping to find a way of entry. To their delight, a window in the old kitchen was part-open due to a faulty latch. Knowing the kitchen was unused and so unlikely to be occupied, they opened the window wide and quickly slipped inside where they hid in a dark corner and listened intently hoping not to hear the sound of unwelcome voices anywhere nearby.

All was quiet and so they left the kitchen and followed the route they had taken earlier with the guide in order to guarantee they would not get lost. To ensure their feet made no sound in the hallway, they both removed their shoes and tiptoed along the wooden floor and the occasional heavy rug. When they saw the window sill with the flower arrangement, they quickened their pace but to their dismay the gun was no longer visible. Determined to find it, Hetty ran her hands behind the curtains and around the back of the large mantle vase holding the flowers but to no avail. Someone had beaten them to it and the gun was not there.

Bitterly disappointed they agreed to abandon the search and make a swift exit before their bravery vanished or they were seen. But as they turned to retrace their steps, the sudden sound of loud voices emanated from further down the passage. Instantly they stopped in their tracks, stood up straight and listened. The voices were coming from a nearby room which because they had viewed it earlier during the tour they knew to be the library.

Curiosity quashed any fear and without hesitation they tiptoed back along the corridor and outside the closed library door, they listened. Inside a woman was talking; she sounded flustered and appeared unhappy. Hetty and Lottie were intrigued, but when they heard the word *murder*, both ladies stifled gasps and sank to their knees. With their ears close to the door and with hearts rapidly thumping, they attentively listened. Another woman was speaking but the conversation inside the library made no sense at all. They heard mention of the inspector, a recently oiled door and then a lamp having been changed. Hetty and Lottie were puzzled and even more so when they heard mention of someone possibly not being who they claimed to be.

"Hmm," whispered Hetty, "I can't see any connection here with Tommy or anyone else for that matter but there's definitely something fishy going on."

Lottie nodded. "I agree, but short of going in and confronting the two women I don't see how we can find out more."

Hetty suddenly gasped. "I've just had a thought. About Tommy, that is. He often talks in an Irish accent, so do you think that might be what they mean by someone possibly not being who they claim to be?"

"What! You mean Tommy isn't a Cornishman at all but is really Irish?"

Hetty nodded. "Something like that."

Lottie looked back at the door. "So who do you think the women are? I mean, neither sound to me like Samantha Liddicott-Treen."

"No idea," whispered Hetty, "although I think one of them sounded a bit like Alison from the Crown and Anchor."

Lottie looked aghast. "Do you think so?"

Hetty nodded. "But I doubt it is her unless she has the night off."

"Well, that's more than possible. I mean, she and Ashley are hardly likely to work all seven nights."

"Of course, in that case she's possibly up to no good on more than one account."

As they spoke, the sound of approaching footsteps echoed along the floor of a distant passage. Not wanting to be seen the two ladies dashed back along the corridor and hid in a dark recess. The footsteps stopped outside the library door. Hetty peeped round the corner and was just in time to see two young men enter the room each carrying a platter of food.

Chapter Twenty-One

When Hetty and Lottie arrived back at Sea View Cottage it appeared that everyone had gone to bed except Bill who was still up and dozing on the settee. He jumped when he heard the front door close and knocked an empty beer can onto the floor.

"Oh, hello, good, you're back," he muttered, stifling a yawn, as they entered the room, "I thought I'd better wait up." He sat up straight. "Is everything alright?"

Lottie, flustered after the cycle ride, forced a smile. "Yes, everything is fine, thank you, Bill."

"Good, good, so, did you win anything?"

Lottie frowned, clearly confused. "What?"

"At the bingo," said Bill, stifling another yawn, "did you win anything?"

Having forgotten that's where they were supposed to have gone Lottie gave a sudden false laugh. "Hmm, no, sadly not. Still never mind, eh." She threw her handbag into a chair. "I take it everyone else has gone to bed," she hastily added, keen to change the subject.

Bill picked up the empty beer can and stood it on the coffee table beside several others. "Yes, they've all gone to bed and no, winning's not everything. So did you have a pleasant evening?"

"Very nice, thank you," Lottie tried not to sound agitated.

Bill rose from the chair. "Good, and were there many there?"

"Oh, err, yes…quite a few," said Lottie, wishing Bill would go to bed.

"Well, I suppose because the weather was nice earlier in the evening that lots of people were having barbecues."

"Barbecues," repeated Lottie.

"Yes, barbecues. Meaning some people who might have otherwise gone to the bingo were probably out in their gardens."

"Oh, yes…I see."

Bill yawned again. "Anyway, I must be off to bed now. Don't forget to lock the door and I'll see you both in the morning. Goodnight."

"Goodnight, Bill," said Lottie and Hetty together.

As Bill left the room Lottie flopped down in the settee that he had vacated. "Bugger, he got me really muddled then. I'd forgotten all about the sodding bingo."

Hetty sat down beside her sister before her shaking legs gave way. "So had I. Just as well the others were all in bed and Bill was sleepy or someone might have noticed there are burrs stuck on the bottom of your trousers."

"What! Oh no," Lottie laboriously began to pick them off. "There are some on yours too," she giggled, dropping burrs into one of the empty beer cans. "Oh what a shocking pair we are."

Hetty looked at her legs. "Damn, it looks like I've torn my trousers too. Must have been when I caught them on that stump of wood as I climbed over the wall. Oh well they can go in the rag bag when I get home."

"Rag bag," said Lottie, "you can't just throw away a perfectly good pair of trousers."

"They're not good, they're torn."

"Well, I'm sure they can be mended. Lift your leg up."

Hetty did as she was asked.

"Yes," said Lottie, "it's just the seam come undone so you can mend them when you get home."

"I don't do mending," said Hetty, banging her foot back down on the floor, "I can't sew straight. Anyway, one can't have too many rags."

"One can't have too many rags," repeated Lottie, clearly annoyed, "Really, Hetty you're so lazy but then you never were parsimonious, not even when we were children. Anyway, if you won't mend them then I will, so when you take them off please give them to me and I'll take them home. They'll be as good as new when I've finished with them, you'll see."

"Okay, okay," said Hetty, leaning back on the cushions. "Don't nag. Besides at the moment we've more important things to discuss than my trousers. I mean, what are we going to do about what we heard tonight?"

Lottie shook her head. "I'm not sure. Right now I can't even think straight. Perhaps we ought to sleep on it and decide in the morning. We certainly can't do anything tonight anyway."

"I agree," said Hetty, rising, "that bike ride has just about done me in. I reckon we were doing thirty down that hill."

Lottie stood and took the beer cans into the kitchen; the sisters then wearily made their way to bed. At first they thought it might be difficult to sleep but the fresh air had exercise had tired them out and they slept soundly throughout the night.

On Wednesday morning, Lottie and Hetty awoke simultaneously and instantly recalled their nocturnal visit to Pentrillick House the previous night. Both looked glum.

"Oh dear, what are we going to do?" said Hetty, sitting up in bed and reaching for her slippers. "This is like some kind of nightmare."

"I think that it is our bounden duty to report our observation of the gun on the window sill to the police."

Hetty winced. "I thought you might say something like that."

"But don't you agree?"

"Yes, I suppose so, but we can't confess to breaking into Pentrillick House last night, can we? I mean, that would be foolhardy especially if there isn't any criminal activity taking place up there." She laughed. "And even if there is we'd still most likely get done for breaking and entering."

Lottie nodded sagely. "I don't think there's any need for us to mention last night. You see, if we tell the police about seeing the gun in the afternoon, they're bound to check our story out. Which means that if there is anything dodgy going on, then surely they'll be adept enough to suss it out without us needing to say another word."

"You're quite right," said Hetty, clearly relieved. "Thank goodness for that."

During breakfast, Lottie casually mentioned that they had seen a gun during their tour of Pentrillick House the previous day and they had decided to report it to the police just in case it was in any way linked to the death of Faith Trethewy.

Bill was flabbergasted. "Why on earth didn't you say anything when you got back here yesterday afternoon?"

"Oh, well, we didn't think it was important," said Hetty, hoping no-one noticed her cheeks turning pink.

"But you do now?" said Sandra, clearly puzzled, "so what's changed your mind?"

Lottie squirmed in her chair. "Um, we um…discussed it this morning, Hetty and I that is, and we agreed it might be of some significance."

Hetty nodded. "Yes, better to be safe than sorry."

Bill tutted. "I'm surprised at you both, especially after all the talk of looking for Faith's killer. You should have phoned the police last night instead of going to bingo. They'll probably think you very careless and who could blame them."

The younger twins looked alarmed. "I can't believe that you saw a real gun," said Kate.

"And that it might have killed someone," Vicky added. "That's gross."

"And scary," said Kate, as Bill looked for a local non-emergency police number on Google.

Vicky agreed. "Yes, but at the same time it's quite exciting."

Bill, having found the number he wanted, went into the kitchen to call the police and within twenty minutes of his call, a police car containing two officers arrived at the cottage. Once they were inside and seated, the sisters nervously explained to them what they had seen during their daytime visit to Pentrillick House. Both police officers seemed very interested in their story and said that they would investigate right away.

To pass away the time until they heard back from the police and to get away from Bill and Sandra who were seemingly still annoyed with the sisters, Lottie and Hetty took a bus into Penzance and visited a gallery where Malcolm Biggins' pottery was on display along with the work of other local artists and craftsmen. To their delight Malcolm was actually there and so they asked how Louise was faring and then chatted to him in a casual manner to glean something of his character. On leaving the premises both agreed that he seemed a perfectly nice and normal man but all the same his name, along with all the others, must still remain on their list of suspects.

After the gallery visit they walked down to the sea front to take a stroll along the promenade and were surprised when they came across a large outdoor swimming pool near to the sea.

"Jubilee Pool," said Hetty, noting its name, "how fascinating. We must tell Sandra about it as I'm sure she'd love to bring the girls down here for a swim."

Following their walk along the promenade they returned to the town centre, having already decided to have lunch before they went back to Pentrillick. As they approached an empty shop with the lights on and the door wide open, natural inquisitiveness caused both sisters to glance in the window. Inside, much to their surprise they saw Doug and Don along with two workmen. Thinking the shop might be something to do with the talked about business venture, they slowed their pace eager to try and establish for what purpose the shop might be intended. Don was at the back leaning on a counter and pointing out something on a large sheet of paper. Doug was kneeling with his back to the window sorting through a box. Suddenly Hetty gasped, quickly took hold of Lottie by the arm and hurried her away from the window.

"Did you see that?" she asked, her hand firmly placed over her chest as though to steady her thumping heart.

Lottie frowned. "See what? I've no idea what you're talking about, Het."

Hetty leaned against the wall of the neighbouring shop. "I'm talking about the tattoo on the back of Doug's neck." She paused to catch her breath.

"Tattoo," repeated Lottie. "I didn't see a tattoo on his neck."

"Well, I did," said Hetty. "It was just one word… *Faith*."

Lottie's face turned pale. "Are you sure, Hetty? I mean, they both have quite a lot tattoos so you might have read it wrong." She stepped away. "I'll go and take a peep."

Hetty pulled her back. "No don't because they might see you. Anyway, I didn't read it wrong. As I said it was just the one word and it was definitely *Faith*. It was clearly visible over the back of his T-shirt neckline."

"Perhaps he knows someone else called Faith," said Lottie, with hope. "It might even be his mother's name."

"Bit of a coincidence, don't you think? No, Lottie, there's more to those two blokes than anyone realises and I reckon they're up to no good." She sighed deeply. "What with those two and the dodgy goings on at Pentrillick House, I feel as though we're surrounded by crooks and murderers."

"Well, there's nothing we can do about it here and now," said Lottie, feeling Hetty was being melodramatic, "so I suggest we go and get some lunch and make a point of looking out for Doug another day when hopefully we'll be able to catch a glimpse of his neck again."

Hetty nodded. "Yes, you're quite right and lunch would be ideal as I'm feeling in need of a sit down. My legs are quite wobbly."

After their lunch they walked along the coastal path to Marazion and from there caught a bus back to Pentrillick. On their return to the village they were surprised to see a police car parked outside the cottage. When they went inside they found the two officers who had called that morning, both seated in the sitting room drinking tea and eating biscuits with Sandra and Bill.

One of the officers rose as the sisters entered the room. "We thought we had better come and put your minds at rest," he said, his face lit with a cheeky grin.

Hetty and Lottie sat down side by side on the settee. Neither could think of anything to say and so they smiled, rather foolishly.

The officer sat back down. "Now, I'm sure you'll be pleased to know that we have been along to Pentrillick House and have spoken to Mr Liddicott-Treen. I have seen the gun you saw on the window sill and it is a replica which is owned by Mr Liddicott-Treen. The reason it was on the sill was because it was to be used later in the day by the local amateur dramatics society, the Pentrillick Players, for their up-and-coming production of Agatha Christie's *A Murder is Announced*. Mr Liddicott-Treen is a member of the drama group, you see, and he had looked the gun out earlier in the day ready for last night's rehearsal which I'm told took place in the library, as is the case every Tuesday evening."

Lottie wished the floor would swallow her up. Hetty tried to keep a straight face but couldn't and so laughed. Bill looked heavenwards.

"I'm so sorry that we sent you on a wild goose chase," said Lottie, feeling the need to apologise, "but I can assure you that our intentions were honourable."

"I'm sure they were," said the older of the two policemen, "and you did the right thing."

"Yep, better to be safe than sorry," said the younger officer.

They both stood up and moved towards the door. Hetty felt she ought to say something about Doug's tattoo but decided to keep quiet as no doubt the possibility of either Doug or Don being involved in Faith's murder had already been explored."

"Thank you for being so understanding," said Sandra.

"All in a day's work," said the older officer. "Good day, ladies, sir, and thank you for the tea and biscuits."

In the early evening, Sandra entered the living room with a pile of washing which she had folded ready for everyone to take up to their respective rooms. As she crossed the floor, her foot caught on the corner of the rug. She tripped, the washing flew up into the air and Sandra fell against the occasional table where Lottie's aspidistra stood. The table tilted to one side, the large pot toppled and then tumbled onto the floor. The room went quiet as the family surveyed the damage. The large replica ceramic Victorian pot lay on the rug broken clean in half and the aspidistra, its leaves twisted and bent, had slipped from its plastic pot and rolled underneath the table.

"Sorry," said Sandra, kneeling to clear up the mess, "I don't think the plant is damaged but the pot is, I'm afraid."

Lottie knelt down beside her daughter-in-law. "Don't be silly, love, it wasn't your fault. Did you hurt yourself?"

Sandra shook her head. "No, no, I'm fine." She pulled out the plant from underneath the table. "Thank you for asking."

"Should have left the cumbersome thing outside or better still at the car boot sale," chuckled Hetty, as she picked up the washing to re-fold it. "Shame about the ceramic Victorian pot though. That was the best thing about it."

Feeling he ought to help, Bill stood up. "Go and fetch the brush and dustpan from under the sink please, Kate." He picked up the two halves of the broken pot. "At least it's a nice clean break so it could be mended with super glue."

Sandra stood the plastic pot upright on the table and dropped the root ball of the aspidistra into it. She tried to push it down but it would not fit. Confused, she lifted out the plant and shook the pot to loosen the damp compost lying in the bottom. As it levelled out, something glinted in a beam of sunlight...something silver. Sandra tilted the plastic pot to one side to see what the something was. The aspidistra slipped from her hands as she screamed and the colour drained from her face. Lying in the bottom of the pot was a small hand gun.

"Don't touch it, love," said Bill, leaping forward to take the plastic pot from his wife, "don't touch it."

"I wasn't going to," said Sandra, sitting down on the floor afraid that her legs might give way.

Lottie looked at her potless aspidistra lying limply on the rug. She was speechless.

Hetty in a state of shock, bit her bottom lip. "Oh dear. I think we need to give the police another ring." She glanced around the room. "Any volunteers?"

Everyone sat perfectly still.

"I'll do it," said Zac, his eyes like saucers, "I mean, this is for real so it won't be a waste of time, will it?"

"Not unless this gun is a replica as well," said Lottie, half hoping it was.

The police were at the cottage within ten minutes...the same two officers who had already called twice that day. They viewed the gun in the bottom of the pot and asked for how long the aspidistra had been in the family's possession.

"Not long," said Lottie, coughing in an attempt to remove the tremble in her voice, "in fact just a week. I bought it last Wednesday at a car boot sale."

"Rosudgeon?" asked the officer.

Lottie nodded. "Yes, it was amongst lots of stuff from a house clearance. I felt sorry for it."

"Hmm, interesting, well, I'm afraid we're going to have to take it away for forensics to look over, but you'll get it back someday."

Lottie looked downcast. "But we go home on Saturday."

"I see. Well, leave it with me and I'll see what we can do."

While one of the officers meticulously wrote down the details of how the plant had fallen and details of its purchase, the other officer carefully placed the gun, the aspidistra, the plastic pot, the compost and the two halves of the replica Victorian pot all into separate plastic bags; he then took them out to the police car.

After the police had gone, Sandra took the rug outside and vigorously shook it, she then vacuumed up the last traces of compost from the carpet while Bill handed out mugs of tea.

Lottie looked at Hetty. "Where do you think the aspidistra lived before I bought it?"

Hetty answered promptly. "Primrose Cottage without a doubt, and that gun was the one that killed poor Faith."

Lottie nodded. "That's what I think but I hope it wasn't."

"Oh no, surely not," said Sandra.

"Well," said Vicky, "if the plant did come from Faith's house and that was the gun which killed her, then my money goes on Rosie Rutherford being the killer."

"Vicky, that's a shocking thing to say," scolded Sandra. "Rosie is a lovely lady and Faith was her friend."

"Hmm, but she could be right," said Lottie. "After all, Rosie was first on the scene and she could easily have hidden the gun there although it would have made far more sense if she'd taken it home. But I don't think it's likely, Vicky. As your mum said, they were friends and I can't see any possible reason for Rosie to have killed poor Faith anyway."

"Well, Rosie certainly wouldn't have done it for the money, would she?" said Kate, "She must be loaded."

"Actually, Lottie and I have a much more plausible suspect, don't we, Lottie?" said Hetty. "Someone with a motive."

Bill groaned. "Oh dear, well I hope you're going to keep the name of the poor chap to yourselves. I think we've had quite enough visits from the police for one holiday."

Sandra nodded. "I second that. Leave it to the professionals."

"No, no, please tell us," pleaded Vicky.

Hetty shook her head. "I'd better not, sweetheart. Not now anyway but I'll tell you when we're all safely back home."

Bill stood up and rubbed his hands together. "Anyway, that's enough about guns and murder. Who's coming to the pub for a bite to eat?"

"Me," said Zac, springing up from his chair, "hopefully some of my friends will be there."

The females all frowned and shook their heads

Bill was puzzled. "Am I out of favour for some reason?"

Sandra tutted. "Really, Bill, you are forgetful. It's the first episode of the *Great British Bake Off* tonight and so we're all staying put and having a pizza."

Chapter Twenty-Two

The following morning dawned bright and sunny and so during breakfast, Hetty and Lottie cheerfully informed the rest of the family they were going out for a nice walk to get some exercise and fresh air. They didn't say where they were going and no-one asked which was just as well because their destination was the charity shop where they were keen to pass on details regarding the gun in the aspidistra pot to their new friends, Maisie and Daisy. However, on entering the shop they were surprised to discover that both ladies already knew of the previous evening's discovery at Sea View Cottage, right down to the very last detail. The sisters were flabbergasted.

"Good, grief, news certainly travels fast in this neck of the woods," said Hetty, sitting down on a box of books. "So, who told you?"

Maisie pointed to Lottie. "Why, this good lady's son of course."

Lottie gasped. "What, my Bill?"

Maisie nodded. "Yes, that's the chap. My Jimmy went to the pub last night, you see, and so was there when your boy arrived with that good looking grandson of yours. Apparently they were both full of the fact a gun had turned up in an aspidistra plant that you'd bought at a car boot sale. Needless to say they had quite an audience as everyone was fascinated. Jim was full of it when he got home."

Lottie's jaw dropped. "He didn't tell us that he'd told anyone, did he, Het?"

Hetty shook her head. "No, but then we'd gone to bed by the time he got back so he might have told Sandra."

"Well, I never," said Lottie. "You know as much as us then."

Daisy folded her arms and winked. "We probably know more."

Both sisters arched their eyebrows.

"Yes," said Daisy, "you see, Tess Dobson was in this morning and she said that Rosie had phoned her first thing and said not to go

145

up to the house today. She does a bit of cleaning for Rosie and Thursdays is one of her days."

Both sisters frowned. "And?" said Hetty.

"Well, apparently Rosie had a visit from the old Bill last night about Faith's death after which they took away her phone, tablet and laptop. And then this morning they rang her to say they were coming round again to question her further. Needless to say, that's why she didn't want Tess there."

"But surely they don't think Rosie had anything to do with Faith's murder?" said Hetty. "I mean to say, they were good friends, weren't they?"

Maisie nodded dramatically. "Yes, and had been for several years."

"So, do you know the outcome of the questioning?" Lottie eagerly asked.

"Not yet, although I believe they're treating her more as a witness than a suspect. On the other hand, it does seem odd that they took away her laptop and so forth and we do know that the gun found in your plant was definitely the one used to kill poor Faith." She paused for a few seconds to reconsider her statement, "At least that's what we've heard on the grapevine, about the gun, I mean. And I believe it's claimed the story originated from a very reliable source."

As they spoke the shop door opened and a middle-aged woman hurriedly stepped inside. "I thought I'd come and tell you the latest," she said, letting the door slam shut. "Rosie just rang me: the coppers have been and gone, you see. Anyway, she's not been charged or anything like that. Needless to say her fingerprints weren't on the gun or the plant pot and I could have told them that would be the case." She tutted angrily. "But they haven't returned her phone, laptop or tablet, which I think is a damn cheek. I mean, they obviously can't muster up a jot of evidence against her because she's as innocent as any of us. Silly sods. Pity they don't go after real criminals and leave the likes of poor Rosie alone. Poor lamb, she sounded really upset."

Hetty cast a questioning glance at Maisie who nodded in response.

"Tess, meet Hetty and Lottie, they're on holiday and staying in Sea View Cottage."

Tess smiled sweetly and shook hands with the sisters. "Pleased to meet you both."

"And ladies, this is Tess Dobson who I mentioned just minutes ago."

"Of course," said Hetty, "it makes sense now. Delighted to meet you too, dear."

"So Rosie is in the clear," said Lottie, somewhat relieved.

"For the time being," said Alison Rowe, the pub's landlady, who heard the last comment as she entered the shop with a box of donations, "although I was talking to Gail in the post office earlier this morning and she reckons there are a few people in the village who aren't too keen on Rosie and that they're suggesting Rosie killed Faith and hid the gun in the aspidistra pot when she saw or heard young Kyle approaching with Faith's cottage loaf."

"Hmm, and I suppose that was the line of thought the police were following," said Lottie. "But it seems a silly notion to me."

"I agree," said Maisie. "Rosie wouldn't hurt a fly and she certainly wouldn't have been after the hidden money, so she had no reason to kill Faith. No motive whatever."

Alison nodded. "That's just what I said to Gail."

Hetty and Lottie left the charity shop and walked back through the village, their heads spinning with the latest gossip. As they approached the church Hetty suggested they take a wander around the graveyard.

Lottie was puzzled. "Any reason why?"

Hetty shrugged her shoulders. "Not really, I just like churchyards. I like the peace and quiet and you can often glean a bit of local knowledge from the headstones."

"Such as?"

"Local names for instance. If one crops up frequently over many years then you'd know they're a family with deep roots here."

"Yes, but that's about all. That and lots of dates."

"Are you being awkward, Mrs Burton?"

Lottie laughed. "I'm trying, Miss Tonkins."

"Anyway," said Hetty, "the tranquillity of churchyards gives one the chance to think and right now we both have a lot of thinking to do, because to be honest, I'm feeling very muddled."

"Snap," said Lottie, watching as her sister opened the large wooden gate.

The graveyard was huge and had obviously been extended several times over many years. The original boundary walls were unchanged on three sides but at the far end, part of the wall had been knocked down to form an entrance into what at one time would have been a field.

Hetty and Lottie sat down on a bench facing north with the church behind. To their left, were various buildings which edged the village's main street. To their right was a lane with access to a row of bungalows.

"I expect Bernie the Boatman lives in one of them," said Lottie, pointing to the bungalows. "Bill said he lived behind the church."

"Yes, he did. I wonder where Tommy and his mum live."

"They're in one of the houses up near where Rosie and at one time Faith lived," said Lottie. "Don't know which one though."

Hetty's jaw dropped. "What, Blackberry Way? How come you've never mentioned that before?"

Lottie looked puzzled. "I thought you knew. Maisie or Daisy mentioned it when we were in the pub on Quiz night. Don't you remember?"

Hetty shook her head. "I'm not likely to forget something like that, am I?"

"Oh, you must have gone to the loo then. I am sorry, Het, but it never occurred to me you'd missed that piece of news."

Hetty leaned forward. "So, if Tommy lives up near Faith then there's even more reason to suspect him of her murder."

Lottie tutted. "Come, Het, be realistic. To be fair to Tommy we don't really know of any reason why he might have killed Faith. Alright, so we saw him come out of a betting shop but that doesn't make him a reckless gambler and even if he is it doesn't mean he has money problems."

Hetty stuck out her bottom lip. "There's still the fact he's a window cleaner and so might have seen Faith counting out the money in her bedroom."

Lottie laughed, but not unkindly. "My dear, girl, we don't even know that he cleaned Faith's windows. Young Barry might have done them or she might have done them herself. I do my own and always have."

"I still think it was Tommy," said Hetty, obstinately. "On the other hand it might have been Doug. You know, I'm thinking of his *Faith* tattoo."

Lottie shook her head. "Well I don't think it's either of them."

Hetty looked smug. "One of us will be proved right, my dear, Lottie."

Lottie smiled. "And one of us will be proved wrong."

They stood up but before they left they decided to take a walk around the new area to see the flowers on Barry's grave. Next to him, at the head of a fresh mound of bare earth, a simple cross bore the name, Faith Trethewy.

"Poor Faith. I hope she'll have a proper headstone," said Hetty.

"In time no doubt," said Lottie, "but they won't erect one until the ground has settled."

While Lottie read the cards on Barry's flowers, Hetty cast her eyes back towards the church and the road.

"Well, look at that, Lottie, you can see our cottage from here, and that window you can see through the trees must be in Zac's room."

As she spoke she suddenly remembered that Zac had on two occasions said he was sure there was someone in the churchyard late at night. She walked around always keeping Zac's window in her sight.

"If Zac did see someone in here then it must have been around this spot," said Hetty, waving her arm to indicate the area, "because his window is only visible in this small patch."

"Probably someone taking a short cut home," said Lottie, bending to smell a freesia, "or maybe they were just admiring the flowers."

"Admiring the flowers. What, in the middle of the night?"

Lottie laughed. "Oh, yes, I'd forgotten that, although didn't Zac say he saw a flashing light? In which case it was probably someone admiring the flowers by torchlight."

Hetty's jaw dropped. "Lottie Burton, have you gone mad?"

Lottie chuckled. "Okay, perhaps that is a bit far-fetched but he could still have been taking a short cut."

Hetty shook her head. "I don't think so. We're nowhere near the path."

"So, are you suggesting that if Zac really did see someone then they must have been up to no good?" Lottie stood up.

"You bet I am, and I'm trying to figure out what."

"But that's ridiculous. What possible mischief could anyone get up to in this spot? There's nothing here other than a few graves."

"Shush, I'm thinking." Hetty stooped down beside Faith's grave and ran her hand over the bare earth.

"What are you doing?" Lottie asked.

"I'm not sure but I've a feeling this earth has been tampered with. Someone has been rooting about in it or something like that. See, it looks disturbed."

Lottie laughed. "Probably a dog has been sniffing round here or some other type of animal. Or it may have got disturbed when they took the dead wreaths away. I think you're getting paranoid again, Het."

Hetty ignored her sister and began to push aside the loose earth.

Lottie was aghast. "Hetty stop that right now. What you're doing is disrespectful and wrong, very wrong. Poor Faith. Let the poor woman rest in peace."

But Hetty continued to sift through the earth and to her delight her fingers touched against something smooth and hard. She dug deeper and pulled the something out. To her utter amazement she saw it was a mobile phone.

For a whole thirty seconds, Lottie was speechless and then she found her voice. "Does it work, Het? Can you see who it belongs to?"

Hetty rose to her feet. "No to both questions," she said, brushing earth from the phone and attempting to switch it on. "It's as dead as a doornail."

"Well can you put some life into it with your charger thing?"

Hetty shook her head. "No, it's a different phone to mine."

"So what are we to do? I mean, it might have belonged to Faith." The pitch of her voice rose. "Oh, Het, both her phone and laptop were stolen. What's it doing in her grave? I think we ought to tell the police."

Hetty laughed. "We ought, yes, but we can't, can we? I mean, how to we explain finding a phone buried just below the surface of a murder victim's grave."

Lottie nervously looked over her shoulder. "I don't know."

"Exactly, I mean to say, they already have us labelled as a bit odd. I suggest we just take it back to the cottage and think about it for a while. As far as I can see there's no rush and I daresay if it's dead or damaged by the damp then the police won't get much from it either."

Lottie nodded. "No, but at least they'd be able to establish whether or not it was the type of phone that Faith owned."

Hetty nodded. "That's true, but knowing our luck if we hand it in to the police they'll most likely establish that it was dropped by one of the gravediggers and I really don't want to have to explain my reason for poking around in Faith's grave anyway. They'll think I'm potty."

Lottie giggled. "Oh dear, what a pickle."

"Come on, let's go back to the cottage. I could do with a cup of tea and I need to scrub my nails."

"Yes, but before we go, I think you'd better smooth that over," said Lottie, pointing to Faith's grave. "It looks like a rabbit hole at present."

Hetty levelled the earth and flattened it with the palms of her hands. The sisters then returned to the cottage with the phone safely hidden inside Hetty's handbag.

Back at the cottage, Hetty and Lottie found Sandra and the girls in the conservatory having just returned from a trip to Penzance.

"We're awarding you ten out of ten for finding the Jubilee Pool," said Sandra, rising from her chair as the ladies walked in, "it's really nice and so we've had a lovely time, haven't we girls?"

"Brill," said Vicky, "I wish we'd discovered it earlier though because there probably won't be another chance to go again now."

"Yes, that is a shame," Sandra agreed, "it was beautifully clean, and of course I was able to sit on the side of the pool and do a spot of sun bathing."

"So is it new?" Lottie asked, as she sat down.

"No, it's quite old apparently but it only re-opened earlier this year after being closed for refurbishment."

"That's because it was damaged in a crazy storm a couple of years ago," said Kate. "Must have been some storm."

"Well the coast is very vulnerable," said Hetty, also sitting, "I must admit I'd like to witness a storm down here. It must be really exciting to see the sea when it's wild."

"Tea?" Sandra asked.

"Only if you're having one," said Lottie.

"Well, actually, I was."

"Then yes, please," said the sisters in unison.

Because there was a vast selection of spices in one of the kitchen cupboards, Bill made a curry for the family on Thursday evening with fish that he had caught earlier in the day while out with Bernie the Boatman. And then afterwards, feeling in need to get a little exercise, they all walked down to the Crown and Anchor where to their surprise they were treated like minor celebrities. Everyone it seemed wanted to sit close to and question them about the gun in the aspidistra. And the conversation for the entire evening focused mainly on the death of poor Faith Trethewy and just who might have taken her life.

As the evening progressed, Doug and Don arrived and joined in with the conversation. Hetty, on first seeing Doug, was hopeful of catching a glimpse of his neck but to her dismay she noted he was wearing a designer shirt and so the back of his neck was completely hidden beneath the collar. They did however establish the purpose for Doug and Don's meeting with the builders in Penzance. The pair owned a small chain of tattoo parlours in various parts of the country and the reason for their stay in Pentrillick for the latter part of the winter had been to look for suitable premises in Cornwall in order to open up a series of shops in the county. While disappointed that Doug and Don had a legitimate reason for their long stay, Hetty still thought it possible that at some time Doug might have returned to the village and taken Faith's life, but she had to admit to herself that she could think of no possible motive. However, when the opportunity arose for her to speak to Doug she seized it eagerly, hoping it might enable her to make a more accurate assessment of his character.

"I keep seeing you and your friend around," she said in her sweetest voice as they stood side by side at the bar buying drinks. "Are you staying in the village?"

"Yep, we're staying at the hotel up the road. Nice place and nice staff too."

"That's good to hear and I believe you stayed in Sea View Cottage for a while last winter. We're staying there now and very nice it is too."

"Yeah, certainly is," Doug agreed. "While we were staying there we actually thought about investing in a couple of holiday cottages here rather than open a few more shops, thinking it might be easy money but in the end we opted for the shops." He chuckled. "I mean, you only have to look at us to see we're more suited to tattooing than we'd ever be for choosing bedding and curtains and women's stuff like that."

Hetty smothered a smile, amused by the image of the two men shopping for bed linen and drapery. To stop herself laughing she turned the subject to Faith. "The poor villagers have had a rough time lately, haven't they? I'm referring to the two recent deaths. Of course, I never met Faith but I did see young Barry and I've met his mother."

Doug paid for two pints and took a sip from one. "Hmm, I met em both." He laughed. "Faith were a smashing looking chic but she wouldn't have anything to do with the likes of me. She said she liked her men to have hair on their heads. Still, each to their own." He gave Hetty a nod and a smile and then went off to join Don who was talking to Bernie the Boatman. Hetty smiled to herself and decided it might be best if she returned her focus to Tommy Thomas.

With a tray of drinks for the family she went back to her seat, hoping that Tommy might call in for a pint or that someone might say something to implicate him, but to her dismay not once was his name uttered nor did he put in an appearance.

Lottie, on the other hand, kept a watchful eye on landlady Alison, hoping that at some time during the evening Vince Royale would arrive thus enabling her to observe the body language between the two. She was not disappointed. For while the rest of family were being informed of yet another version of the morning Faith had died, Vince arrived. Lottie watched carefully. He smiled at Alison who reached for a pint glass. She pointed to the Doom Bar pump and he nodded. She poured the beer and handed it to him. He took some change from his pocket but she shook her head and smiled. Vince raised his glass, winked and said "Cheers."

Lottie nudged Hetty. "Did you see that, Het?" she whispered. "Alison just gave Prince Vince a pint but wouldn't take any money for it. I told you that pair were up to no good."

Hetty frowned. "Really?"

Lottie nodded.

"Hmm, in that case, I think you and I, Lottie, will have much to discuss when we get to the privacy of our room tonight."

When the family arrived back at the cottage just after eleven o'clock, Lottie removed her jacket and hung it on one of the pegs in the hall, but as she walked away the loop broke and the jacket fell onto the floor. Vicky, standing nearby picked up the garment to re-hang it but as she turned it over to sort the top from the bottom, her fingers felt a small object tucked inside the lining. "Grandma, there's something in the hem of your jacket."

Lottie looked puzzled. "Is there? Bring it here please, Vicky."

Lottie felt around the hem. Vicky was right. Something was trapped inside the lining. "It feels like one of those disposable cigarette lighters," she said, as she carried the jacket into the living room and sat down with it on her lap. "In which case it must have belonged to Rosie because this jacket used to be hers."

Hetty scowled. "I didn't think Rosie smoked, but then I've only ever seen her in the pub and of course it's not allowed in there."

"And we saw her at the Pentrillick House," said Vicky, "you know, at the garden party."

"Yes, you're quite right," agreed Hetty, "and we saw her at the car boot sale too."

Lottie still fumbling with the lining suddenly remembered that one of the pockets had a small hole in the seam and so she carefully pushed two fingers into the gap and eased the lighter towards the pocket until she was able to grasp it and pull it out.

"Oh, yes, I was right," she said with a smile. But then the smile disappeared from her face. "Actually, I don't think it is a lighter after all. Look, it doesn't have a clicky thing on the top." She held it up for all to see. "Can anyone help, because I've no idea what it is?"

Kate looked over Lottie's shoulder. "It's a memory stick, Grandma. You plug it into the USB port of a computer and store things on it."

"It's a what?" Lottie's mouth turned upside-down.

Hetty took the memory stick from her sister's hand. "You really should get yourself a computer, Lottie. It'd open up a whole new world for you. You're so behind the times."

Sandra who was signing into her laptop to check Facebook, held up her cupped hands. "Throw it over here, Auntie and we'll have a look to see if there's anything interesting on it."

Everyone gathered around Sandra as she clicked onto the index where only one item was logged; it was titled *Pix pennies*. A list came up on the screen. As Sandra scrolled down the children lost interest.

"Just a list of Rosie's paintings," said Hetty, sitting down on the settee. "How disappointing."

"Hmm," said Sandra, "but it seems a rather peculiar list and why does it have Faith's name at the top of the page."

"Faith's name," Bill repeated, looking over her shoulder, "that does seem odd." He looked down the list which comprised the paintings done by Rosie since she'd been in Cornwall, for each title was of a Cornish beauty spot or tourist attraction. Before each title was a date and after was a sum of money; one thousand pounds in every case and marked as paid.

"So what do you make of it?" Sandra asked, as Bill stood up straight, a puzzled look on his face.

"I'm not sure. I mean, it's obviously a list of Rosie's paintings but the sums of money can't be right as she'd have sold each one for a lot more than a grand."

"Exactly," Sandra agreed, "and for that reason I feel this might be an important discovery."

Hetty, intrigued by the conversation stood up and looked over Sandra's shoulder. She frowned. "You're right, both of you, those prices are ludicrously low for an artist of Rosie's standing."

"I think we ought to hand this to the police," said Sandra.

Bill frowned. "Do you really?"

"Yes, I'm not quite sure why, but I've a sneaky feeling this list has been done by Faith and not Rosie."

"But if it was done by Faith, why would Rosie have it?" said Hetty, "It doesn't make any sense."

Sandra reached for her handbag and took out her phone. "I agree, but because it involves Faith and she was murdered, we must hand it to the police. And for that reason I shall ring them right away."

Chapter Twenty-Three

Late on Thursday evening, an eerie wind whistled around the side of Tuzzy-Muzzy as Rosie Rutherford placed two large bags into the boot of her car. After slamming the door shut she ran up the steps and into her house, glad to get back inside where it was warm.

Being informed by the police of the gun's discovery in the bottom of the aspidistra pot had made Rosie jittery. She knew she was the subject of idle village gossip but also that there was nothing to associate her with Faith's death. After all, the police had returned her phone, laptop and tablet that afternoon because they were all completely devoid of any incriminating evidence and so she knew the endless theories travelling by local jungle drums were pure speculation. Nevertheless, she was nervous and so her undivided attention was focused on gathering together all she needed to make a swift exit from Pentrillick: just for a few days until the dust settled.

Rosie looked at the clock on the mantelpiece. It was fifteen minutes to midnight. From the wall above the fireplace, she lifted down a painting of Pentrillick. It was her favourite. She smiled thoughtfully; the penguins looked so sweet sitting on the beach together beneath a sunshade wearing dark glasses. Faith had liked that picture too. Tears welled in Rosie's eyes but she quickly brushed them away. This was not the time to get sentimental. But then she paused and sat down on a chair by the empty fireplace. What a mess her life had become.

Looking at the painting she remembered the day that Faith had finished it. It was two days before Christmas and they'd gone out for a meal at the Crown and Anchor. Not that anyone knew the reason for their celebration. No-one knew. At least not then.

Rosie first became aware of Faith's artistic talents five years earlier when she had donated a painting called *The Bird Table* to an art exhibition where the paintings were to be sold by auction to raise money for a children's charity. Rosie was one of the exhibition's organisers and from the moment she first saw Faith's work she was mesmerised by her style, her use of colour and the fine detail. So much so, she bought the picture in the auction and hung in a prominent position in her London home.

At the time of the exhibition, Rosie's own paintings were modern; usually of nothing in particular and she gave them the first name that came into her head. Secretly she thought they were unskilled rubbish but for some reason they had become a *must have* collectable item and made her a very substantial living. But Rosie was not happy; her work bored her and her eyes were continually drawn to the birds in Faith's painting hungrily pecking at food on a cold and frosty morning.

On the back of *The Bird Table* was Faith's name. Her address, Rosie found on a list of persons who had donated their work to the charity exhibition. Rosie had never heard of Pentrillick and so she Googled it and discovered a house called Tuzzy-Muzzy was for sale in the village. She read the estate agents' details thoroughly and looked at the pictures. She liked what she saw and so without even viewing the property, bought it and moved to the village, her sole intention being to make Faith's acquaintance.

To Rosie's utter amazement, she discovered that Primrose Cottage, the house next door to Tuzzy-Muzzy, was in fact the home of the very person whose acquaintance she was eager to make…Faith Trethewy; thus she realised the close proximity of the two properties, would be ideal for making their first encounter seem natural and unpremeditated.

To ensure the subject of art arose when their first meeting occurred, Rosie had hung *The Bird Table* in a prominent position in her sitting room confident that her new neighbour would react the moment she saw it. Her wait for that first meeting was not long. The following day Faith had the day off work and so called in at Tuzzy-Muzzy for coffee, following an invitation from Rosie during a brief exchange of pleasantries over the garden wall.

When Faith saw *The Bird Table* her jaw dropped. Rosie, convincingly pretending that she had no idea that her favourite painting's artist actually lived in Cornwall. And Faith, overcome with Rosie's compliments was happy to discuss the subject of art.

But to Rosie's dismay, she discovered that it was ten years since Faith had finished *The Bird Table* and she no longer painted. It was too time consuming, she claimed, and she had a full time job at Pentrillick House which she loved. But shortly after that meeting, Faith had the car accident which was to change her life forever and would cost her the job she so enjoyed.

Once she came out of hospital and was on the road to recovery Faith suddenly found that she had all the time in the world. It was then that Rosie made her neighbour a proposition. Faith had the talent and Rosie had the name, and so if they were to work together they could produce beautiful pictures, ideally of Cornwall. Faith liked the idea; they shook hands on the deal and both agreed it must always be a closely guarded secret.

And so Faith began to paint again; sometimes at Tuzzy-Muzzy but more often than not in Rosie's studio in the old lifeboat house. She never painted at home for fear that someone might see the tools of her trade and ask questions. Because Faith liked penguins they agreed to include two small penguins on every picture and consider it a trade mark.

Everything went to plan. The art world, which at first was miffed by Rosie's dramatic change of style, gradually accepted her work and it became even more popular than her modern paintings, especially to holiday makers who wanted to capture a part of Cornwall and take it home, usually by way of inexpensive prints.

For three years everything went well. Faith produced several paintings a year for which Rosie paid her one thousand pounds each in cash. Faith was happy with that amount for she knew that was far more than she would get if she were to try and sell the paintings in her own name.

And then one day Faith revealed that she had told Barry of their little secret while drinking tea in the garden of Primrose Cottage after he had mowed her lawn. Faith assured Rosie there was no need to worry. Barry was a good lad who had vowed never to tell. But Rosie had worried. Not only would her reputation be destroyed should the truth come out but she might also be arrested and charged with fraud. For that reason Rosie suggested that it might be better if they ceased doing the paintings of Cornwall and that she reverted to her modern art on pretence that the fine detail was a strain on her eyes. Faith took the suggestion badly, she swore at Rosie; called her a string of offensive names and then threatened to tell the police herself of Rosie's scandalous dishonesty should she ever mention terminating their agreement again. Deeply shocked, Rosie promptly ran home her heart thumping wildly. She was afraid; afraid that Faith would reveal the truth to get her revenge, and that was a risk Rosie was not prepared to take.

Rosie had a gun in her possession. A small handgun, illegally gained, which had been given to her by a friend in London who suggested that she keep it about her person to use should she ever feel under threat. Rosie had been appalled at the idea but had accepted the gun with false gratitude, but she had never once taken it out with her and since her purchase of Tuzzy-Muzzy had always kept it safely locked up in the bottom drawer of her writing bureau.

During the morning of the day after Rosie and Faith had fallen out, Rosie frantically rubbed over the gun to remove any of her finger prints. She then, wearing rubber gloves, tucked the gun inside her jacket pocket and crept around to Primrose Cottage. She didn't knock on the door but walked straight in. Faith was in the living room dusting the glass shade of a table lamp. When she saw Rosie she threw the duster into a chair and tried to leave the room. But Rosie was too quick. She pulled out the gun and fired three shots. Faith fell to the floor. Panic-stricken by her actions, Rosie dropped down onto her knees. The gun slid from her hands as she crept forwards and gripped Faith's wrist. There was no pulse. She took a small mirror from her pocket and held it in front of Faith's mouth. There was no breath. Rosie felt sick. Faith was dead and she had killed her.

Stumbling to her feet, Rosie reached for Faith's handbag; took out her mobile phone and dropped it into the pocket of her tunic. She then unplugged Faith's laptop, tucked it beneath her arm and headed for the door. But as she passed the window, she saw Kyle's delivery van pull up on the lane. She needed to get Faith's laptop and phone out of the house for both or either might contain incriminating evidence against her. Quickly she ran into the kitchen and out through the back door where she tossed both over the boundary wall and onto the driveway of Tuzzy-Muzzy. She then remembered the gun lying on Faith's living room floor. She ran back inside the cottage. She had to dispose of it. Kyle was closing the door of the van. Suddenly she remembered that Faith had potted up the aspidistra only a few days before and so she quickly yanked the plant from its plastic pot and buried the gun in the fresh compost at the bottom. With force, she pushed the plant back in its pot, tidied around the edges and then gathered up compost which had flicked onto the table in the duster Faith had been using and stuffed it into her pocket.

As Kyle walked across the tarmac with a loaf of bread in his hand, Rosie quickly dropped to her knees and screamed loudly so that when Kyle walked into the room he found Faith lying motionless on the floor and Rosie kneeling beside her, sobbing.

Rosie told him that she had been gardening, heard some shots, had run in and found Faith dead. Kyle believed her. Rosie scrambled to her feet and said that she must go home and phone the police. On the driveway of Tuzzy-Muzzy she picked up Faith's laptop and mobile phone and hid both temporarily in her dustbin along with the rubber gloves and the duster.

The melodic chiming of the clock on the mantelpiece as it struck midnight brought Rosie back to the present. With a deep sigh she stood up and hung the painting back on the wall. She thought it unlikely the police would have reason to question her again regarding Faith's death. After all they could not link her to the gun found in the aspidistra pot and she believed that there was no other incriminating evidence out there to be found. Faith's phone on which she had stored photographs of subjects she had later painted, and her laptop on which she had listed the paintings done and the sums paid, were both, she believed, back in her possession following a short spell in the graveyard. For after retrieving Faith's laptop and phone from her dustbin on the day she died, Rosie had hidden them in her garden shed. However, a few weeks later she had panicked at the thought of the police bringing in sniffer dogs to try and locate them and so she had gone to the graveyard in the dead of night and buried them briefly in Faith's grave knowing it was the last place on earth that anyone would ever look.

She smiled to herself; all was well. And as for Barry, it seemed the police weren't even treating his death as suspicious. She laughed, recalling the look of shock on Barry's face when he saw the 'missed call' from Faith's phone. At the time she had been waiting, Faith's phone in her hands, hiding behind gorse bushes knowing the route that he took every night with his faithful dog. And while he was still in a state of shock she had rushed forwards and pushed him over the edge of the cliff. To her delight, his phone slipped from his hands as he fell, and so she wrote the contentious message to Louise on Facebook and then tossed the phone over the cliff to join its owner.

Rosie went out to her utility room and pulled out a dirty carrier bag from behind the chest freezer. She peeped inside. "You are both going on a little trip to London," she said, "where you are destined for retirement on the bottom of the River Thames." She then took the bag out to the car and placed it in the boot oblivious of the fact that the phone had fallen from the bag when she had retrieved it from Faith's grave in the dark and it had since been unearthed by two inquisitive ladies. She was also unaware that Faith had copied the list of paintings she had done and her earnings onto a memory stick.

Rosie went into her kitchen, convinced there was plenty of time for a cup of coffee before she left for the long drive. She was after all not on the verge of going on the run but just preparing to go away for a few days to get some peace and quiet in her London home.

As she lifted the kettle and held it beneath the tap, she heard the sound of tyres crunching along her driveway. She put the kettle down, went into the dining room and pulled back the curtains. In the beam of light from her outside lamp, she saw several police officers quickly stepping from inside three cars. Rosie froze and waited for the knock on her door.

Chapter Twenty-Four

Friday morning dawned bright and sunny with a light south westerly wind which seemed ineffectual in its attempt to blow the fluffy white clouds across the endless blue sky.

Along Blackberry Way and inside Fuchsia Cottage, Mildred Thomas shuffled into the kitchen where her son Tommy was making cups of tea for them both.

"Morning, Mum, did you sleep well?"

"Humph, I would have, had it not been for the kerfuffle at Rosie Rutherford's place last night." She sat down heavily in her favourite chair. "I reckon they've taken her in, you know."

Tommy placed two mugs of steaming tea on the kitchen table. "Taken who in where?"

"The police. I reckon they've taken Rosie in. You know, nicked her."

Tommy sat down opposite his mother. "Err, can you explain a bit better than that?"

Mildred tutted. "They were at her place again last night cos I saw them. Three cars there were and dozens of coppers."

Tommy frowned. "Are you sure?"

"Of course I'm sure. It were dead quiet last night, well, there was a bit of wind but no rain to muffle any sounds and so I clearly heard the cop cars crunching up her driveway. Being a concerned neighbour I of course got out of bed, opened my window and took a peep. I could see the cars in the light from her lamp. As I said, there were three."

"What time was this?"

"About midnight."

Tommy was flabbergasted. "So did you hear or see them leave? How long were they there?"

"About half an hour. It was freezing sitting by the open window waiting for them to go. I had to put my dressing gown on but I was still cold." She picked up her mug of tea from the table. "I'm surprised you didn't hear anything."

Tommy shook his head. "I didn't hear a thing, but then I was watching a film and wearing headphones, so that's hardly surprising."

On Friday afternoon, Hetty and Lottie walked down the road for a final visit to the charity shop where they wanted to say goodbye to Daisy and Maisie and to thank them for their friendliness during the holiday. For the following morning they were due to return to their respective homes.

They found the shop door wide open to let in the warm and welcome sunshine. And as soon as they stepped over the threshold, Maisie excitedly informed them that Rosie Rutherford had been arrested and charged with the murder of both Faith Trethewy and Barry Pascoe.

"I'm not surprised," whispered Lottie, "but how could she have been so cruel?"

"Charged with the murder of Barry as well," said Hetty, clearly shaken, "Are you sure?"

"Yes, it was on the local radio this lunchtime," said Maisie, "but we don't know why they suddenly arrested her. In fact at the moment we're completely in the dark. I'm hoping Tess will be in later because surely she'll know something."

"Oh dear," said Lottie, feeling faint.

Hetty quickly guided her sister down onto a green faux leather pouffe which sent its five pound price tag to the floor. "We know why, don't we, Lottie?"

Lottie nodded. "Yes, we do. You see it was in the pocket of the jacket I bought from you on Monday. Well, not the pocket, it was in the lining, although it must have been in the pocket first of all for it to have slipped through into the lining."

"Yes," agreed Hetty, "it found its way through the small hole where the seam had come undone."

"What found its way through a small hole?" Daisy asked, clearly confused.

"A memory stick," said Hetty. "Lottie found a memory stick in the lining of her jacket."

"Yes, silly me," said Lottie, trying to give a little laugh, "I thought it was a lighter, you see, because I'm not up with technology and stuff like that. The family soon put me right though. And of course, you told me that the jacket had once belonged to Rosie, so we put two and two together and it seems on this occasion we actually made four."

"That's right, the jacket did belong to Rosie as I said in the pub the other night," said Daisy, "but I don't know anything about a memory stick."

"Wow, wow, just a minute," said Maisie, "are we talking about the jacket you bought on Monday, Lottie?"

"Yes, the blue three quarter length."

"But that wasn't one of Rosie's, it belonged to Faith."

Lottie gasped, "Faith?"

Daisy frowned. "Are you sure? I mean, it came in with Rosie's stuff."

"Yes, but apparently Faith left it in Rosie's studio a couple of months ago and after she died Rosie asked Mrs Trethewy what to do with it and she said to bring it to us and so Rosie did, along with some of her own things. I only know because Mrs Trethewy mentioned it when I saw her the other day."

"Oh, I'm sorry to have misled you," said Daisy, "but I really didn't know that."

"It doesn't matter anyway," said Lottie, sadly, "I just wish Faith was still here to wear it."

"Anyway, let's get back to the story," said Maisie, "Tell us about the memory stick. I mean, what was on it?"

"Well, nothing much, just a list of Rosie's paintings," said Hetty, "and beside each title was a date and the sum of one thousand pounds marked paid. Which on reflection makes sense because if the jacket was Faith's then the memory stick obviously belonged to her. That certainly baffled us last night, I must admit. I mean, we thought the jacket was Rosie's, and so couldn't understand why she had a memory stick with Faith's name at the top of the list."

"So, are you implying that Faith has been doing Rosie's pictures and getting paid for it?" asked Daisy.

Lottie nodded. "Yes, that's right. The ones since she's been in Cornwall anyway and Faith no doubt kept a record of it on her laptop which would explain why Rosie took it away."

"It also explains the twenty thousand pounds in the knicker drawer," said Maisie, "Well, I never."

"But I wonder why Rosie took Faith's phone?" said Daisy.

"We assume just in case there was anything on it that might implicate her," said Hetty. "You know, pictures or something like that. The police were very interested when we rang them up last night and were at the cottage in no time. It didn't take them many minutes to see what the list meant either, because they'd suspected for some time that Faith was doing Rosie's paintings but they had no evidence."

Daisy slowly shook her head. "So had Faith not put stuff on the memory stick then Rosie would have got away with it."

Lottie nodded. "Yes, it certainly looks that way."

Maisie sat down beside the counter. "So in a way, you Lottie are quite a heroine. I mean, were it not for you buying the aspidistra at the car boot sale, then the gun might not have turned up for years. Likewise, it was your purchase of the jacket that uncovered the memory stick. My dear lady, you damn near solved these crimes single-handed."

"And without even knowing it," said Lottie, with a deep sigh.

Hetty wagged her finger. "Although some credit must go to your daughter-in-law, Lottie. After all, had Sandra not tripped on the rug and knocked over that bloomin' plant then the gun would be going home with you tomorrow and you'd be none the wiser."

Lottie shuddered. "What a horrible thought. Living alone in a house with a gun and not knowing it."

"I've just thought of something else," said Hetty, "I bet the person you saw lurking in the garden a few days back was Rosie looking for the aspidistra. Remember you mentioned at the garden party that you'd put it outside. That must have been music to her ears."

"And I daresay she also went into the cottage on that Friday night for the very same reason, not knowing the poor old plant was camping out for the night. She said that she didn't have a key but she clearly had."

"My goodness, there appears to be more to this than meets the eye," said Maisie, "you've provided us with enough gossip to last for months. I'm very impressed."

"Me too," said Daisy, "You must come here for a holiday again, both of you."

"Now that would be nice," said Lottie.

Hetty suddenly giggled in a childlike manner. "Don't tell him," she whispered, "but for a while we thought your Tommy Thomas might have shot poor Faith."

Maisie's jaw dropped. "Tommy, my goodness why ever would you have thought that?"

Hetty looked sheepish. "Well, you see, we reckoned whoever did it was after the money and so it had to be someone in need. A compulsive gambler maybe or someone reliant on drugs. Anyway, one day when we were in Helston we saw Tommy come out of a betting shop, so we put two and two together and it seems on that occasion made five or probably even six."

"You couple of Charlies," said a voice from behind. All four jumped and when they looked around saw Tommy standing in the open doorway. Hetty and Lottie blushed scarlet but Tommy laughed.

"My sister works in that betting shop," he said, walking towards the ladies, where he dropped down a bag of donations he'd just collected, "and the other day was her birthday. I popped in to see her with a card and a box of chocolates from Mother and myself." He tutted. "Compulsive gambler indeed."

On Friday night the entire family went to the Crown and Anchor, even Hetty, who because of all the excitement decided to forgo watching *Gardeners' World*: besides, it was their last evening.

Needless to say the place was crowded and buzzing with talk of Rosie's arrest and the horror of learning that Barry had also been her victim.

Ashley, delighted at the large turnout, said the family's first drinks were on the house, an acknowledgement that he regarded much of the busyness was down to their bizarre handiwork.

Bernie the Boatman came to join the family and wish them a safe journey home. With him was his friend, Vince, who when close up looked even more like a young Prince Charles.

167

"I suppose for you the season is coming to an end now," said Bill, thinking how much he'd miss his fishing trips.

Bernie nodded. "That's right, it's August Bank Holiday this weekend and it always quietens down a fair bit after that. Although, when the children have gone back to school there's usually a few folks around. You know, mostly couples without children who prefer it when it's quieter." He laughed. "And then of course we get the *Poldark* fans down hoping to see something of the filming that takes place in the autumn."

"So what do you do in the long winter months?" Bill asked.

"Take my ease, do a spot of fishing and enjoy a good long rest. Although of course the Wonderland preparations will be getting underway come early October so that'll take up a fair bit of time."

"Wonderland," said Sandra, "what's that?"

"A Christmas Wonderland, we had one last year in the grounds of Pentrillick House and it was such a success that Tristan said we can do it again." He chuckled. "I was Father Christmas last year and Vince made a sleigh for folks to ride in."

"But it had discreet wheels," said Vince, "because it wouldn't have gone far with runners."

"And did you have a reindeer pulling it?" Hetty asked.

Bernie nodded. "Yep, someone local has a herd of reindeer so we hired a couple from her. Oh, you should have seen it. It was great fun. The kids from the village school put on a Nativity play up there one evening as well and Vince's sister and her helpers did an amazing job with costumes."

"Oh, I didn't know you had a sister," said Hetty, visualising a young Princess Anne, "I take it she lives locally then."

Vince laughed. "Yes, very local."

Hetty was confused by his joviality.

"His sister is our landlady," said Bernie, nodding towards the bar. "The lovely Alison."

In the games annexe, Kate and Vicky were watching their brother play pool with Kyle. To their delight, Zac won.

"Blimey, that was an impressive win," said Emma, giving Zac a quick hug. "Pity you're going home tomorrow. We could do with you on the team."

"We certainly could," Kyle agreed. "I can't believe how much you've improved since we first met you."

Zac was chuffed. "Thanks. I'll certainly continue playing when I get home."

As Kyle set up the balls for another game, Bill brought in a tray with drinks for the youngsters. When he returned to the bar where the rest of the family sat he found a strange man sitting between his mother and his aunt.

"Bill," said Hetty, tapping the arm of the stranger, "this gentleman is Tommy Thomas who helps out in the charity shop, and I'd like to think, in fact, I sincerely hope, that we can call him a friend."

Tommy winked. "You can do that, my darlin'," he said raising his glass, "and here's cheers to the lot of you and I hope we get the pleasure of seeing you all again one day."

Chapter Twenty-Five

Hetty awoke very early on Saturday morning to see the sun shining in through the bedroom window. Promptly, she sat up and then because it would soon be time to leave Pentrillick, she showered and quickly dressed. Leaving the rest of the family sleeping, she quietly unlocked the back door and crept from the cottage and down to the beach.

There was an eerie quietness about the morning. As Hetty stood on the shingle and looked out to sea she realised that no wind rustled the bunting nor stirred up the sea. No voices chattered or excited children screamed. No boat engines roared along the coast, nor gulls cried as they savaged for the remains of picnic baskets and takeaway food boxes.

Hetty walked down to the water's edge and watched as the waves gently rippled and fell softly onto the shore. She sighed. The holiday had been wonderful and she had thoroughly enjoyed spending time with the family. But all good things must to come to an end and now it was time to go home to face another winter in her lonely bungalow.

As Hetty turned and began to walk back across the beach she saw a lone figure walking over the cobbles. As the figure got closer she saw that it was Doug. He nodded politely as he laid down a towel on one of the benches. "Lovely morning," he said, looking towards the clear blue sky. "I reckon today's going to be a scorcher."

Hetty smiled. "Yes, it is and sadly I have to go home."

"Hmm, rotten luck, eh." He glanced across the empty beach. "I love it down here when it's so quiet. There's a sort of magic about the place."

"I agree, I wish I could capture this moment and take it home with me." Hetty asked, eying his towel, "Are you going for a dip?"

"Yep, nothing like a nice swim while I have the water all to myself."

Hetty sighed. "I think I envy you."

With a chuckle he kicked off his flip-flops and removed his T-shirt. Hetty turned to walk away but then paused when she heard him speak, "Hope you have a safe journey home and perhaps we'll see you again one day."

"Thank you. And I hope your new business venture goes to plan."

He crossed his fingers. "Yes, we hope so too."

As he turned towards the sea Hetty saw a string of words tattooed down the middle of his back. They said: *Faith in oneself is the best and safest course. Michelangelo.*

Hetty's jaw dropped. What a fool she was. But she managed to refrain from laughing until she had climbed the steps and reached the garden gate.

The family were all up and sitting round the table when Hetty walked into the dining room.

"There you are, Het," said Lottie, pulling out a chair from beneath the table for her sister, "we were beginning to wonder where on earth you'd disappeared to."

Hetty sat down, "I just went down to the beach. You know, to say goodbye."

Sandra looked up sharply, aware of the emotion in her aunt's voice. "Oh dear, are you not looking forward to going home?"

Hetty blinked quickly to prevent her eyes from watering. "Not really, this holiday has been wonderful and I've really enjoyed the company of all of you. It's silly, I know, but having been in a family environment these past three weeks has made me realise just what I've missed. Living alone all these years, I mean. I thought I enjoyed my solitude but on reflection I'm not so sure that I do."

"Well, we must do something like this again," said Bill, slicing the top off his boiled egg.

Lottie laughed. "No pressure then, Sandra. It's up to you to win another holiday."

Sandra grimaced. "I'll do my best."

"I'm quite looking forward to going home," said Kate, spreading peanut butter on a slice of toast, "the holiday has been fun but I'd like to see my friends now."

Vicky nodded. "Same here."

"How about you, Zac?" Bill asked.

"I'm torn between the two. Yes, it'll be great to see my mates back home again but I shall miss my new friends here too."

"But at least you'll be able to keep in touch," said Hetty, "technology and the internet make things like that so much easier nowadays. Not like when we were young, eh, Lottie?"

"What time is your train?" Bill asked, glancing at the clock on the mantelpiece.

"One o'clock," said Hetty, "so we've plenty of time yet."

"I'll naturally run you to the station," said Bill.

Hetty paused before she answered. "Well actually, I was thinking it might be nice to catch the bus. It terminates next to the railway station so that's ideal. It'd save you turning out as well. I mean, you already have a long enough drive ahead of you and we all have to vacate the cottage by eleven anyway. What do you think, Lottie?"

"Yes, suits me. I really don't mind either way."

Bill frowned. "Are you sure?"

Both sisters nodded.

"In that case we'll take your luggage with us," said Sandra. "There's plenty of room in the Volvo and it'll give you both a free hand then."

Hetty's face lit up. "If you do that, then we'll be able to get off the bus in Marazion and walk into Penzance along the coastal path. It's a lovely walk, isn't it, Lottie?"

"Absolutely," said Lottie, "I think that's an excellent idea, especially as the weather is simply gorgeous today. In fact probably the best day we've had."

"Typical," muttered Sandra.

"Hmm," said Bill, "I'm not quite sure what the weather's playing at. Bank Holiday weekends are usually wet, cold and miserable."

After breakfast Bill washed up and tidied the kitchen while everyone else packed up their belongings and tidied their rooms.

Lottie and Hetty packed their cases quickly, eager to catch the next bus which was due in twenty minutes. When the job was done, they stripped their beds and carried their luggage downstairs and stood it by the front door.

172

"Have a safe journey home," said Lottie, hugging each member of the family in turn, "and don't forget the aspidistra, will you?"

"We won't," said Sandra, eying the plant which the police had returned the previous day. "In fact I'm sure Bill will mend the planter for you when we get back because we have some super glue at home."

"Yes, I'll do that," said Bill, glancing at the two broken halves on the coffee table.

"And make sure you put things securely round it so that it doesn't topple over," said Hetty, "because we don't want the poor thing damaged."

Lottie's jaw dropped. "But you don't even like my aspidistra. In fact you've said some pretty unkind things about it."

"Yes, well I've had a change of heart. I mean to say, that poor plant has had a very distressing time, hasn't it? First it witnessed the murder of its owner and then it was forced to sit on the murder weapon. After that it was bundled into a van and taken away to a car boot sale. Next you bought it and put it outside in the wind and the rain, and then a few days later it was knocked over and fell from its pot. And as if that wasn't enough it was then arrested and taken off by the police for forensics to poke it around. So, you see, I have the greatest respect for your plant and you'll never hear me say another word against it."

"When you put it like that," said Lottie, "then I can see why it's commonly known as the cast iron plant."

"Hmm," hummed Bill, "anyway, time's getting on so you'd better get off. I hope you have a good journey too and I'll drop your luggage round to you both in the morning unless there's anything you'll need tonight."

"No, that's fine," said Lottie, "there's nothing I'll need for a while."

"Same here," said Hetty, as she too hugged the family.

Lottie and Hetty were both surprised when the twins voluntarily gave each of them a kiss for usually they were reluctant.

"That's because we're proud of you both," said Kate. "You know, solving the murders and all that."

"Yep," agreed Vicky, "I can't wait to tell my friends how cool my gran and great auntie are. They'll be well impressed."

Lottie felt her heart flutter. "Goodness me. I don't think anyone has ever thought of me as cool before. I'm quite chuffed."

"Your bus will be here in five minutes," said Sandra, glancing at her watch. "Better hurry."

Lottie reached for the front door handle. "Yes, come on, Het, we must make a move. Goodbye everyone. Thank you so much for your company and we'll see you tomorrow."

The bus was on time and the sisters sat upstairs, although not at the front as those seats were already taken. Hetty felt a lump in her throat as they passed by the charity shop, the Crown and Anchor and the school before the bus finally left the village and turned away from the coast towards the main road, where as they drove by the garage, they saw Vince and Alison standing outside his bungalow chatting.

"I can't believe that I was daft enough to think ill of those two," said Lottie, quietly tutting, "but it simply never occurred to me that they might be siblings."

"Yes, it doesn't pay to jump to conclusions," said Hetty, thinking of Tommy Thomas and Doug, "because it's all too easy to end up believing one's own guesswork."

As the bus wound through the narrow street of Marazion, the sisters made their way down the narrow stairs and got off the bus when it stopped at The Square where they bought ice creams before making their way through Marazion and onto the coastal path.

As they neared Penzance Hetty reached out and clutched Lottie's sleeve.

"Let's sit for a while and soak up the atmosphere. The train doesn't leave for over an hour yet and we're only fifteen minutes away from the station."

They left the path and climbed over enormous boulders. When they found one with a smooth surface they both sat down.

The sea was flat calm and the water glistened in the sunlight beneath the cloudless blue sky. Gulls squawked as they glided over the beach where people walked and sat enjoying the beautiful, warm weather. From beyond the railway tracks the gentle hum of traffic on the main road hung in the air and mingled with the voices of cyclists, the occasional bark of a dog and pedestrians walking the coastal path.

"A penny for your thoughts," said Lottie, aware that her twin was unusually quiet.

"I was just thinking that if my house was worth more than it is, then I would sell up and move to Cornwall," said Hetty, wistfully. "I've really enjoyed our stay here. I love this walk and I loved Pentrillick and its people. It's daft, but I feel that I belong down here even though I'd never heard of Pentrillick before Sandra won the holiday." Her eyes filled with tears. "I don't want to go home, Lottie. I really don't."

Lottie was shocked. Many years had passed since she had last seen her usually strong willed sister cry. "Don't cry, Het: although I know how you feel. There's a sort of magical feel about the place, isn't there? After living inland all our lives I suppose we're rather bewitched by the sea." She gave a little laugh. "And these three weeks have been rather extraordinary."

Hetty sighed. "Yes, they have. Oh, if only I could win the Lottery. Just one hundred thousand pounds. That's all I'd need to make up the difference between house prices here and at home."

Lottie turned to face her sister and then spoke slowly and thoughtfully, "Winning the Lottery might not necessarily be the solution, Het." She paused. "I mean, if you could bear to share a home with someone else after all these years. Someone who you know quite well, then that someone, being me, could sell up as well and then we could buy a nice little house here together."

Hetty gulped. "What…but…but wouldn't you miss Bill and the family? And what about Hugh's grave? I know you like to take him fresh flowers every week."

"There's no reason why I wouldn't still see Bill and the family. I mean, I could keep in touch on your Facebook thing and they could come to visit too. They'd like that. Besides, they have their own lives to live, and now I'm a widow I suppose I ought to do the same. You know, stand on my own two feet and be independent. I'm sure that's what my dear Hugh would have wanted and as for his grave, I don't doubt that Bill and Sandra will still take him flowers but perhaps just not so often and only in the summer months."

Hetty brushed away the tears with the back of her hand. "Oh, Lottie, I've gone all goosepimply. Do you really think we could pull it off?"

Lottie's face broke into a broad smile. "I don't see why not, Het. My house is far too big for me now anyway and so I ought to move and I can think of nowhere else I'd like to live more than here in Cornwall." She linked arms with Hetty. "And to be honest, there's no-one I'd like to share a house with more than my older twin sister."

More tears emerged and trickled down Hetty's cheeks. "It'd be like old times."

Lottie nodded. "Yes, very old times."

Hetty suddenly gasped. "We could have a dog, Lottie. We could have a dog. As I said the other day, I've thought about it a lot since I gave up work."

"I should like that too."

Hetty looked out towards the sea. "Oh, Lottie, if everything worked out right we could be back here in time for Christmas and be able to go to the Wonderland thing at Pentrillick House."

"And see in the New Year with our new friends."

"And go beachcombing after a winter storm."

"And go blackberrying and make jam."

"I can dye your hair any colour you want."

"And I can mend your clothes, whenever you tear them."

From behind on the railway track they heard the sound of an approaching train. They stood and watched as it slowly passed by and pulled into the station.

"That'll probably be our train," said Hetty, picking up her bag, "so we'd better make a move."

"Yes, time to go home and make plans."

"Exciting plans."

And with arms linked the sisters walked to the station, chatting of their future.

"And wherever we live," said Hetty, her voice part-drowned out by the sound of another train pulling into the station, "the aspidistra will have pride of place."

THE END

Lightning Source UK Ltd.
Milton Keynes UK
UKHW021958090223
416682UK00013B/1412